DESCENDING
*F*IRE

& OTHER STORIES

Also by John Allman

JOHN ALLMAN

DESCENDING
*F*IRE

& OTHER STORIES

3 1336 03619 8605

A NEW DIRECTIONS BOOK

Some of these stories previously appeared in *The Antioch Review* ("Losers and Gainers," Fall 1992), *Epoch* ("The Tip," Spring 1968), and *New Directions in Prose & Poetry 54* ("The Tower," 1990).

Book design by Sylvia Frezzolini
Manufactured in the United States of America
New Directions Books are printed on acid-free paper.
First published clothbound by New Directions in 1994
Published simultaneously in Canada by Penguin Books Canada Limited

Library of Congress Cataloging-in-Publicataion Data

Allman, John, 1935–
    Descending fire & other stories / by John Allman.
        p.   cm.
    Contents: The tower—A chronic case—Courtship—The tip—
Sisters—Losers and gainers—The substitute—Descending fire.
    ISBN 0-8112-1274-2
    I. Title. II. Title: Descending fire and other stories.
PS3551.L46D47   1994
813'.54—dc20   94–6746
                                                       CIP

New Directions Books are published for James Laughlin
by New Directions Publishing Corporation,
80 Eighth Avenue, New York 10011

CONTENTS

for my brother
Dan

THE TOWER

1959

It was called a rendering plant, but Benjamin referred to it as the glue factory—a final place in a corner of Long Island City near the little bridge that goes over into Brooklyn. Each night, since Ace Brown's death, Benjamin climbed to the top of the water tank, standing on the pie-shaped, tapering roof to sight the stars. He wondered how much of Ace had traveled through the giant auger, the Screw, which drove everything into the rendering boiler. If he thought about his own feet being drawn into the blade, if he remembered how he'd found Ace slumped over, he felt a sudden terror of heights and forced himself to peer down into the yard behind the unloading dock, where the white dust drifted out of the window of the bone mill. He grew calm looking out over the plant, allowing himself to remember his mother. "Why don't you live here? Always running around. You don't look good." Later, he would try to read, between doing his rounds as night watchman, muffling the drone in his head of his therapist Leo Reister's voice. "Doing nothing is still a decision." Or he'd stare across the yard at the No Smoking signs above the tallow tanks and think of his girl, Faith Gudrun, her frosted hair and thin lips and small teeth, her body that received him with a largeness belied by her timid nature.

1

Tonight, he felt good looking down. Ridges of the tank's roof gave him footing, though a patch of galvanized metal was stained and uncertain—rust being washed into the grooves from somewhere—and Benjamin was careful to step around it. White smoke rose from the stacks of the rendering boiler on the other side of the yard. There was the window with the broken pane through which he could see into the plant, tracing the path Ace Brown had taken up the slippery staircase before he had fallen into the open Screw. Benjamin had known that one of the metal stairs was loose where it was bolted to the girders on each side. He had found it that afternoon, almost slipped on it as it tilted beneath the pressure of his foot. He could have told someone. Called the front office. Found Mack the timekeeper. The next day he had said to Reister, "If you were a priest, you could mouth some mumbo jumbo and I'd feel better."

What a stupid thing to say, he thought. Ace was dead. Ground up. He could still see those bloodshot eyes, still inhale the smell of cloves on Ace's breath that masked the beer he'd had with lunch.

"If you wasn't white," Ace had once said, "you wouldn't be foolin' around here pretendin' you wanta be here when you know you can leave anytime you want."

Benjamin had wanted to say, "What has color to do with anything?" Wasn't he poor himself? But he knew that Mack never sniffed his breath the way he did the black workers'. That was just good sense, he thought, since they worked heavy machinery.

"I got my troubles, too," he'd said to Ace.

"Yeah. Tell me about it, Jim."

"Maybe you were angry with him," Reister had said. "Maybe you wanted him to fall." He'd been direct like that before, when Benjamin had confided he wanted to begin a career in music. "You're too old, you know. No one makes it in the music world starting at your age." Benjamin had stormed out of the office, feeling betrayed, and felt no better when Faith told him that if he wanted music he should at least pay his electric bill and have the power restored for his hi-fi. But he went into a rage. He didn't want to *make* it. Or be bled by Con Edison. Pushed around by Reister. Now she too. It was belittling.

The stars. There were men preparing to travel into space. It was the end of a decade, hardly a year since Sputnik I had decayed in its orbit, punctured the atmosphere, and blazed back to earth. He could see Orion so clearly from this height that he seemed to lift out of his body, traveling through his eyes, something, his soul, free of his heavy, corpulent needs. He could smell the putrefaction rising from every inch of the plant's works, the odor he'd gagged on that first evening when Mack showed him how to insert the key into the timelock at each station—flanges revolving on a cylinder. Unless he plugged the key into the right station in the right sequence, the flanges would not line up and fit the final station. And an alarm would go off at the security office somewhere in Brooklyn. It was surprisingly serious work, though as an action it was simple-minded, clear, something he could do while he memorized a Wagner libretto, just what he wanted for the long hours. He enjoyed the systematic clicking and lining up of the flanges, the regularity and finality of fitting the key into the last station of the sequence. At least now he had an income.

He could stop moving in with his mother every time he quit a
job or lost an apartment. Besides, she no longer recognized
him anyway. How could a woman not even seventy lose so
much of her memory? It was temporary, Reister said, probably
the result of her sister's death, so that Benjamin's mother,
finally alone, plunged deep into the past, beyond the time he'd
been born, beyond even her marriage, though she would talk
about that nice young man, Otto Kirsch, the carpenter,
though she could still do her own shopping in the grocery store
on 9th Avenue. But where did it leave Benjamin if his mother
in reliving the past had gone so far back that she'd erased him?
When he came to visit her, he would look out at the sparrows
settling on the fire escape where his mother put out slices of
stale bread. How she managed to remain so plump, when she
didn't seem to eat, was a puzzle. If he asked her whether she'd
eaten, or if she needed groceries, she just shuffled back and
forth in her housedress, hair disheveled, and waved at the
sparrows pecking at the bread.

"Ask them," she said, "what they need."

"Mother, you must wash, at least that."

"You. Who are you? You're crazy."

He shook his head, balancing himself on the tank roof, and
with both hands swept back his long, thinning hair, the kind
of motion a conductor might accomplish just before tapping
his baton on the music stand and lifting his hands for the hush
and gathering-in that preceded the first explosion of music. He
inhaled deeply. It was not a good sighting tonight. The moon
was bright, but the cloud cover was getting heavy and the sky
becoming opaque, milky. He descended the ladder on the side
of the tank, holding tightly to the steel rungs, wondering, as

he scraped his foot on each rung to be certain it wasn't slippery, why he hadn't warned Ace about the loose step. Had it been simply that vagueness in his nature that so oppressed Faith at times? An absent-mindedness, as if he left the material world always to be shaped and controlled by others. Someone would fix the stair. Or report it. Or take care going up to the third floor, not looking back down into the Screw.

He stood now on the cement platform that supported the girder-legs of the water tank. He couldn't help seeing the broken window across the yard and, through it, the staircase. No. He wouldn't think about Ace tonight. He would choose what to think about, just as he had chosen where to live, to escape his mother and his fear that something must be wrong with him, to not have to hear about her visits to the nursing home, how his aunt had looked better, or worse. And if Con Ed had removed the gas meter and shut off his electricity in his apartment on 7th Street because he had refused to pay a back bill that was not his but the previous tenant's, that was still a choice he was making. For a year he had been living on canned foods, fresh fruits, kielbasa from 1st Avenue, sometimes going around to Avenue C for one of the specials at Zina's Lun-cheonette; at night using candles and an antique hurricane lamp, when he read the *Paideia,* Werner Jaeger's classic work on education in ancient Greece.

At first, Faith said it was very romantic. It made him such an individual, she said, and he'd felt lucky that they'd met in the church choral group where he hoped his deep baritone would find the training it needed. It was Faith who listened to him describe the life with his mother, the guilt—though he never called it that—he seemed born to. Faith who had sug-gested her own therapist, Leo Reister, a man who seemed

interested in one's soul, not one's money—though Benjamin
soon found that Reister insisted on a token payment, smiling
in his pasty-faced way, talking about his own expenses and
Benjamin's commitment. And it was Faith one night by can-
dlelight who slipped off her clothes and gave herself freely to
Benjamin, Faith who later, while making instant coffee over a
Sterno stove, told him that it was the first time she'd ever felt
safe with a man. And the next morning, Benjamin had felt
good, thinking maybe he would go back to college.

But that had changed. Faith complained of having headaches in his apartment now. She said Leo—and Benjamin always felt jealous when she referred to Reister by his first
name—had praised her for being able to have a relationship.
Even her job as a receptionist for a plastic surgeon was going
well. But maybe she was hiding, she told Benjamin. Maybe
she and he were both avoiding truth. "Just what the hell is
that!" he yelled. And she said he frightened her when he ex-
ploded like that. It was true that he still had not paid Con Ed,
still could not visit his mother, and seemed to work more hours
than ever at the plant, but he needed time. And now she was
giving up on him. Why? He wondered if Reister were stirring
up trouble by talking to Faith about his, Benjamin's, problems. If Reister were competing with him for Faith. But he
hadn't voiced any of his thoughts, and Faith hugged him and
apologized and said that intimacy frightened her and that sensitive people needed to be protected. He had thought she
meant him. Now, looking down on the plant, he realized that
she had been referring to herself.

There was the unloading dock. In front of it, the pyramids of
animal bones attracted anything that lived on carrion or fed on
the scavengers themselves: flies, water bugs, rats, an occasional

dog, and cats, dozens of cats. Above the dock, a constant cloud
of dust poured from the open window of the bone mill, issuing
golden and mealy in the lights that illuminated the bone hop-
per. A man wearing a mouth mask to prevent the inhalation of
bone dust was covered with the fine powder that settled on
everything. He was like a man in a sandstorm, Benjamin
thought, and he felt the work was somehow heroic. Next to the
bone mill was the warehouse, the back of which opened onto a
narrow stream that separated this rendering plant from another
industrial complex, a chemical plant, whose works emitted
their own odors, acrid, sulphuric, that singed Benjamin's nostrils. A tall steel tower at the edge of the stream, overlooking
the warehouse and almost the same height as Benjamin and the
water tank, would shoot out a flame at regular intervals, light-
ing the sky, the rendering plant yard, and the inside of the
warehouse, suddenly casting a red glow on a maimed cat hob-
bling toward the bone mill or the rat he saw now scurrying
alongside the tallow tanks.

It had been the slippery surface, not the looseness of the
step. Ace had known about the slickness of everything one
touched or walked on in the plant. The pipe-railing was loose,
so that while climbing the stairs and tugging the railing, one
expected first a kind of sway, then resistance. The stairs led to
the third floor, and below them was the Screw, an endlessly
turning steel auger as wide as a man's head that churned animal
flesh through a pipe and into the rendering boilers on the third
floor. Up there, the boilers heated everything, and pipes carried the liquified matter like melted shortening down through
various filters floor after floor, until it oozed or gushed into
underground storage tanks. It had been Ace's job to oversee the
proper working of the Screw, opening the strategically placed

trough-lids to clean out the fallen rags or rodents or cats that had mysteriously been crushed into service. In studying the accident, Benjamin calculated that the angle from mid-stairs into the open trough of the Screw was about forty-five degrees—gravity alone being a sufficient force to pull a man down into the clotted, churning blade if the trough-lid was open, if the man slipped and went backward, if the pipe-railing gave way. Or if a man was too tired or too drunk to grab at something, to hang on. But he hadn't warned Ace. The eighth step loosened, bent, slippery, wobbly. How so? There was no rust under all that covering. Water just rolled off. His own spit just rolled off. Filth, dust, soot, cat hair, rodent hair clung to the blackened surface of the stairs. But the bolts locking the step to the slanted beams on each side had been loose. Because a man loosened them? His head ached. An accident. Just an accident. A black man named Ace Brown had fallen into the Screw. Up to his hips before the machinery shut down.

Benjamin walked across the yard to the timekeeper's shack where he had to turn the key in the last time station. He found a cattle skull on the ground and kicked it aside. Why not, he told himself. This, or a human skull, that same bony mansion and eyeless vacuity that any rodent might explore. He thought of Faith. Had she yielded out of pity to him? If he was depressed now, it was really the other side of anger. At least Reister had taught him that. "It's the mirror image of yourself." He turned the key with all its flanges in the time station. The light would flash on at the security office, a man like himself, bored, alone, would be checking off a box in a spiral notebook. "Is that it?" Reister had asked. "Not to compete? You seem to be looking for some kind of test." Benjamin had insisted that one could live without gas and electricity, with-

out the usual needs. He would unlearn things, he'd said, and
Reister had replied, "Then why do you feel this way?" Now he
couldn't keep Faith out of his head, here, in a corner of the
scalehouse, the cats prowling, always a scuffle or scream somewhere in the plant. He remembered the moles on her bare
abdomen like dark points on a constellation chart, as he ran his
hand over her womb, imagining it was already curving, dis-
tended. "One time?" he said. "I know I'm pregnant," she said.
She looked away. "I know what I have to do." He clenched his
jaw muscles. "Life isn't sacred," he said. "It isn't."

He brushed away the flies settling on the brown paper bag
containing his lunch. He put it in the desk drawer, out of
reach. Still they settled, discovering it, clustering on the lip of
the desk, finding it. As he had found Ace, already unconscious,
the man's scream still reverberating throughout the plant. Had
he acted quickly enough? The off button of the power box was
already depressed, punched in, and he saw that Ace had probably been able to reach it there above the open trough-lid at the
same moment he knew it was too late. Benjamin had turned
away from the blood, the terrible precision with which Ace had
been drawn into the blade, feet, ankles, pant cuffs, then his
legs. Ace was leaning sideways against the lid, as if asleep, his
right arm folded under him in the absolutely limp way of the
dead. An emergency siren was blasting upstairs on the third
floor, signaling that the Screw has been shut down and that the
boilers needed adjustment. Ace seemed jammed into a pipe.
Perhaps his legs were merely perpendicular to his spine. Benjamin thought that one could simply lift him up and his legs
would follow, however mutilated. He forced himself to look.
Blood filled the immediate area Ace had descended into, but

Benjamin could see the bright curve of the blade flush with
Ace's groin. Wherever they were, his legs were no longer legs.
All of these observations had taken only a second, though
Benjamin now, remembering it, sorting it, felt it must have
been five minutes before he'd hit the fire alarm and called the
security office.

He leaned back in the timekeeper's chair, where he'd first
seen Ace with his feet on the desk.

"I'm looking for Mack the Timekeeper."

"Baldy? He's roun' back. You looking for work, Jim?" He
laughed.

He seemed to fold and unfold himself as he stood up, tall,
lean, a man about forty, flecks of gray in his hair, his cheeks
sunken, eyes red from drink or fatigue, his skin dark enough so
that his palms were a vivid contrast to the backs of his hands.
"Don't let him put you on no double shift," he warned, almost
mockingly, wagging his forefinger. He exuded a kind of authority and directness that Benjamin admired, and when Benjamin said, "Is that bad?" Ace laughed again and patted him
lightly on the back. "Oh, man, I'm jes kiddin' you." It was
clear that Ace was tired. Benjamin had not yet learned about
the size of his family, the sister and her children, the wife
working in the Bulova factory.

He'd known everything they might say, so he didn't mention college. He told the man in the personnel office—who
seemed to have no interest in how the job got filled—that he'd
just come in from Chicago and read the ad. He invented employment in that city, saying he'd been laid off a job involving
aircraft parts—realizing too late that he should have said he
was from the West Coast, if he'd been working for the aircraft
industry, or he could have said the Republic plant on Long

Island (which they could have checked too quickly for him to
be safe). But none of it had mattered. Following Ace's directions, Benjamin found Mack, the bald, red-faced timekeeper
who just nodded, grunted, asked him for his social security
number and what hours he could work. His mouth curved
downward in a kind of disdain, and he tilted his head and
rolled his eyes, as if to say, "Another winner! Only this one
thinks he's from Chicago." Benjamin's stomach had flut-
tered. He'd almost said, "I'm sorry. Just forget it. Never
mind, goddamn it." But he'd needed rent money. And Reister
had said, "Okay, I'll charge you only ten dollars a visit until
you're on your feet, but you have to get a job or I won't see you
at all."

How many jobs could he quit in a year? There'd been the
bank, that too a night job, mopping floors, cleaning bath-
rooms, taking the overtime workers down in the freight elevator. Before that he'd walked all over Manhattan for a messenger
service, entering immaculate offices and delivering manila
envelopes marked "Urgent" to beautiful young secretaries
who sometimes smiled. And he'd leave, filled with rage,
looking down at his scuffed shoes, his old and shiny gabar-
dine pants given him by a friend he no longer saw, painfully
aware too that the filling in his front tooth was discolored
yellow.

It was Mack who'd asked, pointing to the loose step, "You
know anything about this?" Ace had been cut out, bandaged,
and they had carried him away on the stretcher, holding up a
bottle of plasma that trickled fluid into the plastic tube now
inserted into his wrist. "How can he be alive?" Benjamin had
thought.

"No," he'd said to Mack. "It was okay last night."

The flies settled on his hands as he ate the sandwich. He flicked them off with a twitching motion. He ate, his right cheek reacting spastically to the incessant activity of the flies. Why would anyone kill Ace? Perhaps it was someone's idea of a joke. Just loosen the step . . . and whatever happened would have been funny. Like a pratfall in a silent film. A Chaplin routine, a worker twirling his wrench (as he had in *Modern Times,* chasing the woman with two boltlike buttons on her dress, like huge nipples, going after her with the wrench, trying to tighten her nipples, and Faith had not laughed, while Benjamin was doubled over with laughter, and Faith had said, "It wouldn't be so funny if he could do it to you," and she'd accused him of reacting only to pain or to what could cause it).

What had Reister told Faith about him, and what had he accepted from that man? A man divorced, too involved with his patients, too involved with himself. A man Benjamin had trouble focusing on: soft, his thin hair combed over to one side and separating into strands that showed pink scalp. A man who said, "Because you must choose. Why else had you come to me? You want me to take your head apart and then put it back together and send you home." And when Benjamin said he couldn't remember his father, Reister said, "You keep saying that as if it's important. I don't think so. How can you remember someone you never knew?" An industrial accident. Kirsch the carpenter, who had no business at the site on Pier 81 when they were still doing steel work, struck by a girder that had begun to twist on the cable like a slow propeller, as the crane lifted it to the third story. And Kirsch was knocked off, already dead by the time he disappeared into the oil-slick water. No union. No benefits. For days, Benjamin's mother had walked up and down 9th Avenue between the vegetable market and the grocery that gave her credit, buying items one at a time, a can or an apple, keeping herself busy, always looking north, uptown, shading her eyes, as if her husband were due any minute. Only two shy men with chapped hands and wind-reddened necks had come to the funeral. Something bad going on at the docks, but what? And even these details seemed more what his mother had told him than anything *he* could remember.

"I can't explain it," Faith had said. "I thought I was pregnant. Maybe I had a miscarriage. Leo said it was because . . ." Why did she always call Reister by his first name? She went on about *her* trauma, the brother dead in childhood, the fear of children, the need to replace a lost sibling, the mother who criticized her all the time, as if something had been Faith's fault. She went on, as the afternoon sun struggled through Benjamin's dirty windows. He looked down at the workshoes he wore six days a week, the soles edged with black grime.

After Ace's accident, after thinking Faith was pregnant, he'd stopped fixing birth-beds for the pregnant cats, had, in fact, begun shouting at the cats whenever they approached or tried to rub against his leg. He'd begun grinding his teeth in his late-morning sleep, and as Faith talked, as he listened to her compulsive, breathless recitation of what had created her need to see Leo Reister, his molars ached, and he opened his mouth and worked his jaw from side to side. "I'm glad," he'd said, "we don't have to find an abortionist."

It was time to do his rounds, to roam through the rendering plant and feedhouse, turning the key in each box that rotated another flange into place. "I wouldn't be here now if I had me some college," Ace had said in his direct way, as if always comparing himself with Benjamin. As if upbraiding him. Then he laughed and shouted an order to Louis, his helper with the missing front tooth and freckled mulatto skin. "Hey, you dumb shit, you can't jes keep puttin' it on and off like that. Like this, see?" He took the steel prod from Louis, who had immediately begun to sulk, and as the Screw turned, he caught a bit of rag and flicked it out with a filliplike motion of the prod. "You got to keep the Screw movin' or they gonna have my ass. Not yours. Mine." And Louis had said, "Sheeut." And Ace turned to face Benjamin, as if he were the other adversary, saying, with little humor in his voice, "Man, what you hidin' out from? I mean, what the hell you doin' here, Jim?"

Louis was in charge of the Screw now, and Benjamin was still surprised to see that red-blondish head where he had always seen Ace in his old Brooklyn Dodgers cap. He listened for the whistling, the cursing and laughter, but all he got was Louis' grin, the gap in his teeth. Ace had had gambling debts. He'd resisted the union organizers because the plant manager every month gave him a bonus off the books, just to keep the union out—something Ace had confided, as a way of explaining that he didn't need anything but his wits to make a living. "I got it up here, see?" He'd pointed to his head.

Now, Louis' grin was becoming an open, draughty smile as he stood back from the spinning Screw, the trough-lid closed, holding the long steel prod upright. Ace had always talked, chattering as he cleaned out the Screw, or as he told Louis this one time, quick, to shut it down, or to climb the ladder that led to the feed-pipe's shutoff valve. Louis had been out sick that day. Perhaps Ace had climbed the ladder and fallen from there.

So then it wasn't the loose step. It was Ace in a hurry, trying to do the job of two men, dropping the precautions, slipping off the ladder, falling feet-first into the Screw. And when Benjamin found him unconscious, that too had been an accident, since he was there in the afternoon that day only because Tim the day man was out sick and Mack had sent a telegram asking Benjamin to work a double shift. Had Louis set it up? The loose step. The sick day. Had he been bullied once too often by Ace? Or had he been paid to do it because Ace had enemies at the loading dock who wanted to go union and Ace had spoken against it. "Ain't nobody goin' to tell me what to do!" And the two loaders, who had been seated on the platform, leaning against the wall, got up and spat at his feet. Louis had grinned, and Ace said, "What you grinnin' at, you half-breed."

On Thursday, his day off that week, he visited his mother, bringing a load of dark bread from a bakery on First Avenue. "This kind, you can live on," he used to say, holding up a hemisphere of dense bread with one hand, a serrated knife in the other. Then he would berate American-made white bread. It wasn't money she needed, she used to tell him when he proffered a five-dollar bill. It seemed true enough. Her Social Security checks, a small annuity from her sister's estate: enough for rent, food, the fluffy cat that always scratched Benjamin because he ignored the little growls and rubbed her haunches until she turned on him. And when he told his mother how he was doing at school (a lie only for the moment), how he was creating his future, she would sigh, look out the window, through the fire escape, and say, "I know. Don't I know what you need?" Two years ago she had begun talking about her life, how she'd worked in the Hotel Edison as a maid,

or in the Hotel Astor as an elevator operator. How her father
had been such a handsome man, with his German accent, how
he could fix any machine, how Otto Kirsch had called at the
apartment one day looking for her father. Benjamin had admired the tenderness of those memories. But one day, he'd
come to visit, and she'd said, "Who? I have no son." She didn't
seem to be ill in any way. She simply avoided his eyes, canceled
his existence, because she had decided to ignore not only her
sister's but also her husband's death so long ago, remembering
only how Otto Kirsch had come to the door that one time. And
now she refused to see a doctor. She wasn't destitute. There was
nothing Benjamin could do.

"Perhaps she can't relive the shock of your father's death,"
Reister had said.

"After all these years?"

"Aren't you doing the same thing?"

"Oh, it's you," she said. Dressed in a long terry-cloth robe
with a belt tied on the hill of her abdomen, she stepped back,
holding the door ajar, as if admitting someone inevitable
whom she had no desire to see but whom she had no energy to
resist. She took the bread that Benjamin thrust before him. He
remembered Faith telling him that one shouldn't eat food han-
dled by negative people. It had a charge, a psychic contamina-
tion.

His mother sat down at the formica table Benjamin had
known since childhood. She seemed tired but clear, her hair
short and brushed back, only partly gray in spite of her sixty-
eight years. "I think I've been sick," she said. "Aren't they
cute?" She pointed at the sparrows on the fire escape squab-
bling over a crust of bread. The cat was crouching at the edge of
the window, switching her tail, making little birdlike noises in

her throat as she opened her mouth, lower jaw trembling.
"You stop that!" his mother said. She went over and swatted
the cat, who cringed, then she picked her up, soothing her.
"Oh, I didn't mean that, no, I didn't."
    "You seem fine to me," Benjamin said.
    "Have I been unpleasant to you?" she asked, her round face
no longer with that puffed, tormented look.
    "No. Do you know who I am?"
    "Oh, don't be silly, Otto."

He had to act, he thought on the IRT express that took him
to Fourteenth Street, where he changed for the local. He had to
act. Out of stubbornness he had forced Con Ed to shut off his
electricity. Daylight and candles were all he needed. He had
put newspapers down on his floor and replaced them one day
with carpet remnants discarded by a store on Avenue A. He
laid the squares down in a free-form mosaic in his living room
that now changed acoustically when he sang, and his only real
possession, his hi-fi assembled by hand from a Heath Kit, was
still useless because he had no electricity. He kept his windows
shut in summer to keep mosquitoes out and the tambourines
and singing from the Pentecostal Church in the old store with
the windows painted green and a crucifix painted brown on the
door. Sacrifice. Always that. He imagined Ace hung from a
cross. His body transported on the assembly-line belt leading
upward into the feed storage house. Ace's voice sounding
within the water tank: where Benjamin stood, sighting the
stars, assigning identities to each pinpoint of light. Dreams.
Symbols. As if he himself were a symbol whose meaning
shifted in the minds of the several people important to him.
    If Ace's fall had been an accident, it was in a world without

intention or design. It was death like life: a randomly linked
sperm and egg, gratuitous as a loose brick falling three stories
to fracture the skull of a man putting out his garbage. So he
inspected the ladder. The rungs were slippery. But not from
the blackened fat imbedded in the stairs, clinging to railings,
coating even one's voice. It was a clear greasy substance that
smelled like petroleum jelly. No. More like gas-station lubricant. The plant had its own garage and mechanics. They
worked in the grease pit near the scalehouse. The grease gun
always hung on the eye-hook in the pit, while the compressor
was always humming into action because there was a leak in the
airline. So if the compressor went on suddenly, it wasn't because someone was using the grease gun. And Louis could have
greased the rungs the day before, knowing that Ace would have
to climb the ladder alone at least several times. There had been
no way to examine the soles of Ace's shoes that had been
ground up by the Screw. So Benjamin could only speculate:
either the loose step; or the ladder. He would never know. He
felt his life run before him, like an animal he pursued in a
dream.

Tim was out again, and Mack asked Benjamin to work a
double shift: the scalehouse from three to seven, then the
rounds of the plant from seven until eight the next morning. Then he could have two days and one night off. No choice.
He would work here for three more months, through the summer, then go back to school. His two college years weren't
enough. No degree. No real trade. He'd pick up his Greek and
German and philosophy. Live on state loans. Reister was right.
It was time.

  "I have nothing against you," Faith said. "You think I

invented the pregnancy and then undid it because I've changed
how I feel about you?" Her hair was up in a bun as they walked
through Tomkins Square Park, her milky skin almost reflect-
ing the sunlight. "It's your guilt you're talking about. Yours.
Sometimes I think you live inside a tree."

He worked the truck scale. First, he recorded the tare
weight printed on the side of the truck. Then he pushed up the
lever that released the hand sweeping over the face of the scale.
Then he subtracted the tare. The scalehouse was a little cinder-
block room built into a corner of the garage, near the front
door. Occasionally, late at night, the bell would ring, and he'd
have to come to the scale. (Once it was a pickup truck carrying
a dead racehorse covered with canvas, its rear legs sticking
out.) In late afternoons, there were no rounds to make. He
stayed in the scalehouse until seven, weighing up the last
trucks returning from the butchers at the far end of Queens or
Brooklyn. He knew some of the men, the drivers and their
helpers. Some of the helpers he'd seen at the unloading dock
that day Ace had spoken against the union. They just nodded
or flicked a cigarette out the window.
    Around five o'clock, he saw Louis approaching. He walked
slowly, clapping his hands before him and whistling. His eyes
were small, squeezed between his heavy brow and fat cheeks.
He grinned. His missing tooth had been replaced by a bridge,
and Benjamin could see the metal clips snapped onto the surrounding teeth.
    Louis waved. "What you doin' here, Ben? Where's Tim?"
    Benjamin told him he was out sick. "I have to work a double
shift," he said.
    "No kiddin'. Bet you don't get no ovahtime either."

Benjamin shook his head. He asked Louis how his helper was working out now that Ace . . .

"Sheeut," Louis said. "Ain't nobody good as I was."

Benjamin was repelled by the way Louis leaned over and leered into his face. He could still remember Ace saying, "I had me some college you wouldn't catch me here nohow. You sure got your eyes in backwards."

"You got to open your mouth more, like this, see?" Louis was demonstrating how he played tunes on his teeth, by snapping his fingers one after another like the hammers of a xylophone, controlling pitch and key by making his mouth cavity small or large. "Maybe you ain't used to openin' your mouth wide enough."

"Could be," Benjamin said.

"But that ain't always a bad thing." Louis grinned. His eyes were almost squeezed shut by his fat cheeks. His paunch hung over his belt, nearly obscuring the decorative buckle. The tongue of the buckle was shaped like a king cobra's head, which matched the ring on Louis' left hand. Benjamin stared at the buckle and the ring and almost smiled. Louis' costume effects were so obvious. But they were part of the style that Benjamin was only just beginning to observe in Louis, who had been so anonymous in his dirty workclothes, climbing the ladder or sweeping the floor or rolling out the drums filled with bits of filth he and Ace had extracted from the Screw.

"I went to the funeral," Louis said. "I didn't see you there, but I guess I understand that all right. They wouldn't want no white man there anyhow."

A truck pulled onto the scale, and Benjamin went into the scalehouse, wrote down the tare weight, took the gross weight from the scale face, subtracted the tare, and recorded the net. Louis was asking the driver's helper for a cigarette. The helper gave him a filtered menthol, and Louis grimaced, but took it. The truck pulled away, and Louis tore off the filter. He lit the remaining stub and exhaled the smoke into the scalehouse, where Benjamin had sat down in front of the scale. "This a sweet touch, ain't it?" he said. "Jes sit on your ass. They ain't ast you to join no union, has they?"

Benjamin shook his head.

"Well, if they come roun', I'd be real cautious if I was you."

"Thanks," Benjamin said.

"You an' me, we know what it's all about, don't we?" Louis said, taking a last drag on the cigarette burning small between his fingers.

"You think so?" Benjamin said.

"I know so!" Louis said. He dropped the smoldering butt to the floor and stepped on it, grinding it into the floor.

"Anytime they want, they can take you, like that." He snapped his fingers and grinned. "They's real bad."

"Why should they bother me?" Benjamin said. He'd finally said it, brought it out into the open.

"Cause they mean, real mean," Louis said, leaning over and prodding Benjamin in the chest.

"We'll see," Benjamin said, and pushed Louis' hand away.

"You jes do that," Louis said. Then he left.

It was almost nine o'clock, and he was reaching the fourth station of his rounds, in the poultry feedhouse on the first floor. A rat scurried behind the burlap bags piled on a skid. Him. He wouldn't scurry. It had to be thought out. He had only just so much time. If he could wait it out, avoid Louis and the others, the faceless others Louis alluded to, he'd be free of it all by September.

He climbed the stairs to the second floor. More bags piled on skids; the chute down which the bags would slide to the loading platform. Then the stairs up to the third floor: the opening in the wall where the belt brought the bags upward, across, over the yard, on the girder bridge, to dump them here. Then the ladder to the roof. The catwalk over to the water tank. The ladder up its side. He was on top. Just so much time. He could hear the belt running below him. It clicked and hummed, carrying nothing, an empty treadmill. Like the world turning in a vacuum. Like him turning around and around. He walked the ridges of the roof to where it peaked, and he stood on the tip of the roof that slanted down on all sides. He noticed a white, new section of galvanized metal—someone had repaired that scaled, rusty area. He balanced himself on each side of the peak. The flame shot up from the tower on the other side of the warehouse. The evening was clear, and he could see the blackness curling away from the tip of the flame. There was Orion. The Hunter. He reached up. He wanted to touch Orion's belt. If he could only just touch it, a pinpoint of the infinite.

The flame shot up again, illuminating the yard, and he observed a bright blob of something only inches from his feet. It was grease—like the lubricant he'd found on Ace's ladder. His first thought was that the tinsmith doing repairs had left it, not bothering to look behind, not wiping it off with the omnipresent rag all the workers carried in their rear pockets. But what did metal and welding solder and flux have to do with this type of grease? Had he stepped two inches to the left. . . He felt as if someone had opened a door in his skull.

If the slippery substance had been deliberately placed here, what bothered him more than the thought of his accident was that someone had been observing him closely enough to know his habit of climbing to the water tank. He practiced moving his foot toward the grease. He imagined the slide down the tank roof, the momentary airy sensation of floating in space as he fell toward the yard, just as Ace must have experienced, just as his father must have felt descending toward the river, aware of the numbing area in the back of his head where the girder had struck him, before he blacked out, before he hit the water. Benjamin pulled his foot back, suddenly frozen, suddenly afraid. Anger seemed to fill his hands. He clenched his fists, raised them over his head, and began shouting obscenities, the belt humming, clinking, turning around and around on its endless and unnecessary job, as his baritone boomed out over the plant yard.

$\mathcal{A}$ CHRONIC CASE

1959 / 20??

Since he had met Danielle, a convict like himself, Victor sometimes fancied that back in 1959 his wife Ida had not left him but that he'd thrown her out of their small apartment on Davidson Avenue. And he'd shot the right man. He certainly couldn't forget coming home early that hot June. With her back to him, her recent weight loss evident in her diminished waist, Ida had turned to look over her shoulder like someone just pinched in the behind, her blouse and bra strap slipping down her arm. His brother-in-law Solly, also looking over Ida's shoulder, was just as startled, his right hand on Ida's breast. "Shit!"

Victor remembered that later his daughter Wilma came home from night classes and complained there was nothing decent to eat. All he'd felt was a heaviness in his feet, a thickness in his tongue. For two years, Wilma had been going to Baruch College after work, taking the El home to the apartment in the Bronx, where her parents had tried to be unobtrusive. When she did homework in the living room, they stopped watching TV, mumbling instead at the kitchen table over something in the newspaper. Ida would read the ads and remind Victor that none of his cousins had helped him get his own business. They would argue in whispers, until Wilma blurted out from the other room, "Must you?"

When the judge had asked him where he wanted to serve his sentence, in the present or the future, Victor thought it was just a dream he was having on the cot in Riker's Island, in the cell with the bad-smelling car thief. Danielle said the same thing about thinking she was in a dream, a tremor running through her entire small body. "Yes! I was certain any minute my mother would wake me and tell me I was late for work!"

He still wore his molded, black orthopedic shoes, at an underground refreshment stand in the 14th Street Rapid Transit Station. The station was also a switching hub, and the corridor that had once connected the Canarsie and Lexington lines was now a gleaming passageway that linked commuters to the Downtime and Uptime transports. Victor's stand was in the middle of the passageway. His graying hair had thinned to a kind of tonsure, and one could see a moistness on his balding crown when he removed his paper hat under the lights that bled heat and glare. One still had to descend metal-ridged stairs and wait for platform extensions to slide out before boarding the transports, which resembled the old subway cars.

Each January, in what seemed like his and Ida's apartment on Davidson Avenue, up the hill from Jerome Avenue and the elevated transport that screeched like the old El, a new calendar appeared on the kitchen table. He'd put on some of his old records, Ida's favorites—Mario Lanza, Jan Peerce, Richard Tucker—and remember how he'd shot Cosimo, his daughter's lover, replaying the scene in minute detail, seeing anew the open-mouthed surprise of the man he'd caught in mid-gesture, Cosimo's prominent eyes bulging, the quiver of his lower lip stilled in a freezing instant of disbelief. (Later, in the Detention

Center, the public defender—a bewhiskered man dressed in a
Victorian coat and looking like Disraeli—said, "We have a
motive the jury will love. Insult to family.")

He remembered that after her mother vacated the apartment, Wilma had started visiting friends on City Island. She
took fewer courses, and without her mother to goad her ("You
want to live like this all your life?") finally stopped taking
classes altogether. She talked about moving out. She had gotten wild looking, her hair flaming out in a great mass, the
music she played in her room louder, frantic. She complained
of boredom. When she returned from an overnight stay on City
Island, the odors of turpentine and solvents suffused her
clothes. Sometimes Wilma's hair smelled like oregano. She
told him about Cosimo, who was doing a series of nude portraits of her.

Returning home every evening via the Downtime transport,
finding himself alone in the apartment, under his arm a daily
paper whose news he could not comprehend—all the place
names seemed wrong, even the cities referred to as being on the
shores of the Hudson River—Victor often felt no regrets for
having stood his ground with Wilma. (He should have done
that with Solly years ago. Ida had said, "He didn't talk nice to
you." She meant Solly's sneer whenever Victor talked about
business—though what did Solly know about business, being
himself just the deli man in Olinsky's Supermarket?) Many
nights now Victor lay awake, remembering the scenes with his
daughter, her complaints that he knew nothing about art or
literature. She had brought home two of the portraits done by
Cosimo, the first one showing her as a classical odalisque,
reclining on a couch with broken springs. In the other, her
body had become stylized, her facial expression simplified by a

few lines representing eyes, nose, mouth. He became alarmed. Was this how the man sees you? A cartoon? She began screaming. She brought two more pictures home for him to see, both more realistic, in which she seemed blowzy, dark hollows around her eyes, her lips curled in a thin smile. What now, a whore? She said he was just too ignorant.

A week later, she brought home three pictures. Cosimo had stylized her again, this time reducing her to a series of straight lines, then something curved, something like a blue bowl, then in the last picture she became a swirl of paint—thick lines, spatters—and Victor tried to visualize her beneath the turmoil. It was then he visited his friend Stanley, who ran the candy store down near Fordham Road, and borrowed his .22 revolver.

Victor took the bus to City Island, found Cosimo in his studio on the bay, and shot him three times in the chest. When asked why by the police, all he could say was, "He destroyed her. He debased her. He devoured her. He was no good." (He couldn't remember that interrogation without visualizing Solly, Ida's body half-twisted around, Solly's baggy trousers slightly elevated by an erection.) Wilma wrote him a letter, saying something about the future, about being where he would never find her. He had crumpled it up later, after his sentencing, and thrown it against the wall, from which it bounced into a half-open dresser drawer that still contained his wife's underwear. Even now, the dresser stood against the wall, next to the old phonograph.

Twice now he thought he'd seen Wilma rushing past his refreshment stand among the commuters. Her long red hair, indistinguishable from her mother's at that age, had flared among the dun and dirty blond heads, but when he called her name, coming out from behind the machine, gesturing with an orange in his hand, the woman jogged deeper into the crowd. Once, while working behind the units under which people held their collapsible cups, he saw a woman's hand with bitten-down fingernails like Wilma's. He rushed around to the front only to find a convict dressed like himself in canvas pants, a coarse, sleeveless blouse the color of butter almond. A fidgety, birdlike woman, she was having difficulty inserting her cup under the frozen-custard spigot while also moving along. The result was a slop of custard down the side of her hand and blobs of it on the floor. Rushing past, while also selecting custard or juice, and inserting one's cup, these were many reflexes composing a single skill. It was what made Victor at first believe that the future belonged exclusively to the young.

Sometimes, thinking of Ida, he remembered something about an argument over business; he and Ida on one side, Ida's sister Eve and her husband Solly on the other. Usually, with Eve in the bathroom, Solly would be at the table, shaking his head, saying it was almost impossible to live with her, and Ida would be patting his hand, saying it was a pity she couldn't take a pill or something. "Like arsenic?" Solly would say, and Ida would slap his wrist, "Oh, you!"

He wondered if, several weeks before walking in on Ida and Solly, he'd made the wrong decision when he agreed to take a joint holiday with Solly and Eve and spend several days in Ventor, the community south of Atlantic City. Solly was trying to buy into Lou's, the finest Jewish deli/restaurant (with booths) on Ventnor Avenue. *That* was the argument over money Victor had been trying to remember. Ida had precipitated it when she said that Solly ought to consider ways to let Victor into the investment. Eve had turned on her, saying

Victor had had his chances. Solly had talked dismissively to Victor, out of the side of his mouth, half smiling, his teeth gleaming. "Maybe you could work behind the lunch counter." Later, Ida said, "He didn't talk nice to you." She kept her back to him while she did the dishes, and afterward in bed sighed heavily without saying good night. There would be no holiday, and Ida had said, "Why didn't you tell him to go to hell? Why did I have to say, 'Forget it, we're not going on any holiday with you'?" But then why, he still asked himself, would she let Solly into the apartment, nearly into their bed? Was it a tribute to his brother-in-law's skill (his dark good looks, his boyish eyes, his perfect teeth, his melodic baritone—a man who had married Eve before she became manic and dropsical), or was it Ida's anger at him, Victor?

Solly must have come back that afternoon—perhaps he was on a break from his job at Olinsky's, just a few stops up the Jerome Avenue line—and tried to apologize to Ida. He blamed the argument over the trip to Ventnor on Eve (but carefully, not to offend), who had turned bitter over their lack of children, who mocked him because she knew he fooled around but couldn't prove it. Or pretended she couldn't, and that fueled the manias she brought with her to Davidson Avenue, where she slapped the kitchen table, her upper arms shuddering. "You think that Senator McCarthy would have lasted five minutes if people like you and Victor didn't say, 'I don't have anything to do with that'?" "We lost a lot of money because of him," Ida would say. "Money? What money? You mean all of Papa's money that you wasted on chestnuts?" Eve would throw her hands up in the air.

Victor imagined that afternoon, the knock on the door, Ida answering, Solly with sliced corned beef and pastrami wrapped

in brown paper. Solly offers the cold cuts, his head slightly
bowed. He smiles in the shy way that causes a woman to
believe him sensitive. His glance seems to sweep the floor. He's
looking for how he can push her to the couch. Or into the
bedroom. "Ah, life's too short," he says, insouciant and boyish, a lock of hair falling across his forehead because he uses a
shampoo and a conditioner that keep his hair soft and fluffy for
a woman to run her fingers through. He comments on how thin
Ida has become. How attractive. His hand runs up and down
her arm. He pushes against her. Ida seems too tired to resist.
Too fed up with her husband. Too annoyed with her sister.
And the front door opens . . .

For a long time, Ida had been giving Victor that pitying
smile, the sort he'd grown used to at family gatherings when
his brother Albert and uncles, aunts, and cousins had wondered if something in the family's genetic stock had atrophied
in him. He worked at such a low level in the food business.
Albert had a deli in Mt. Vernon, near Yonkers. All of Victor's
cousins had, one way or another, been in foods. Zina ran Zina's
Coffee Pot at the Brooklyn docks and owned the luncheonette
on Avenue C. Selwyn and Murray ran the candy and drink and
checkroom concessions in Broadway theaters. When he shot
Cosimo, whose work gave him such headaches, it had been, he
now realized, like shooting one of his smiling cousins.

The woman who wandered over to the refuse bin where
Victor had piled Ida's things was the same woman who'd been
unable to capture custard in her cup at the auto-spigots. Next
to the bin, dressed in her convict ivories and whites, she un-
rolled Ida's scarves, held up the panties against her body,
laughed at the bras and put them back on the ground.

Behind a nearby post, Victor was catching his breath. The strain of bringing Ida's things here, of emptying out her dresser, had been great. He peeked around at the woman sorting through the clothes. She was short, wiry, her auburn hair caught up in a bun.

She saw him watching. "These are yours, aren't they?"

"Not quite," he said.

"I don't need to steal."

"God forbid!" he said.

She visited him the following Wednesday evening, after he closed up his stand, shuffling/sliding in his shoes, his shoulders rounded with fatigue.

"Danielle," she said, folding her arms. Radiant in her small, nervous way, she had loosened her hair and replaced the regulation convict canvas outfit with a black skirt. She must have been one of the specials, with privileges.

"What?" He straightened himself the best he could. "What?"

"My name!"

Before he knew it, they were chatting away and he asked her to come home with him. For dinner.

She was quite startling among the damp, worn workers and the gloomy adolescents returning home from distant schools. The workers reached for paper towels on the rollers that retracted into the train wall, and they wiped their faces, and stuffed the used towels into their pockets or purses. Victor lifted his chin up from his chest and smiled as Danielle talked hurriedly about a poem she had been writing that day. There was something heedless about her, something raggedly emotional, and he was thrilled by the poem but afraid to offer an opinion. It had been the cause of much bitterness between him

and his daughter that he had presumed to judge Cosimo's art.
So he just smiled and nodded, as Danielle whispered her poem
above the loud silken hiss of the transport. A worker in blue
frock leaned their way and tried to hear.

It was just then that Victor looked down the car and saw a
red knot of hair that could belong only to his daughter. He
shrieked and began waving his hands, but she slipped out of
the car at the next stop, 149th Street, where the old Court-
house had been, and he was unable to get off in time.

Danielle held him by the elbow. "What?" she said. "What?"

"I saw my daughter!" He reached for a paper towel and held
it to his face. He sobbed briefly.

"It'll be all right," she said. She resumed reciting the poem,
this time making changes that she said she'd later read into the
recorder.

Victor only nodded.

When they got off at 176th Street, as they mounted the
stone stairs that led up to Davidson Avenue, he saw two youths
studying them from a distance, and he had the uncanny feeling
that they were truly back in 1959, but he and Danielle slipped
into the vestibule and he opened the inner door with his key.
They took the capacious, noisy elevator to the fourth floor. The
bright little scarf that Danielle wore round her throat displayed
designs—squiggles, triangles—and colors like those he saw in
the transport ads. He wondered why she'd taken Ida's things if
she wasn't going to wear them, and he began to feel uneasy.
Once inside the apartment, Danielle flopped on the little red
sofa, then wandered over to his record collection and the phonograph. She told him about living with her nearly deaf
mother. She talked about her hope in high school to become a
writer, before her father died. Before she'd taken jobs meant to

be temporary, all of them close to the apartment she shared with her mother. She even told him how she detested her brothers, who lived in California and were the apples of her mother's eye. Victor was aware only of her presence, of the fact that he'd brought a woman home. He could smell the rose water she'd splashed on her throat. She talked about how she had been approached by the deli man in the supermarket that day she asked for lean corned beef and the man said he had some in the storage refrigerator in the back. Maybe she wanted to look first, before he brought it around.

Victor grew pale.

"What is it?" She peered at him, eyes glittering. Any moment she seemed ready to peck at something on his cheek.

"I just realized that maybe I have to go back. I mean, what if my daughter is really ninety years old? What if she stayed behind and aged normally? What if she's dead? What if I'm just seeing her because I want to see her? And that woman on the transport is just something out of my heart that I want to see? What if she died with nothing changed between us? My God." He lowered his face in his hands, and she stroked the fuzzy back of his neck.

"Then I'll just have to go back with you!" she said.

"What if they won't let you go back that far, past 1964, when they sentenced you? What if you disappear, vaporized, zing, gone? What if time tears you apart?"

"Maybe I don't care." She lowered her head and stared into her lap.

"But if you can come back with me, then we can go forward together, in the normal way, to the year you left."

"But what," she said, "if I go back to your time and then five years later do all over again what I did to get me here?"

"What if you go back and don't kill anybody? All this will be forgotten because it never will have happened."

They were overwhelmed with doubt.

"It'll be different. I'll be with you!"

What if he had to relive Ida's departure, Wilma's relationship with Cosimo, the murder of that man? What if Danielle was not who she pretended to be?

"Don't worry so much," she said. "You worry too much." She finished her story, sometimes twitching her head nervously, laughing oddly. She had gone with Solly to the storage room, his white apron stained with salmon-colored streaks. He'd pushed her against a sorting table where someone had left a utility knife that she groped for. She slashed his throat. As he bled to death on the floor, she was already composing ways to tell her mother. And she knew the opening lines of the poem she would write:

> The swift blade to his heart that could not feel,
> sharpness from my tongue, this hot awareness . . .

The detail in the poem of Solly being cut to the heart, rather than across the throat, troubled Victor. It made her seem careless with the truth. But she threw herself into his arms, and he forgot everything.

For several weeks, they traveled back and forth together, Danielle giving up her coupons for the underground shelters (she'd been sentenced to be homeless), sleeping with Victor on the little red sofa. They were perfectly happy. He believed that soon they would shop for a larger bed. He assumed that he would continue to work at the custard stand. Danielle would put her things in Ida's bureau. He had almost given up seeking his daughter. What difference did it make what he had done in 1959?

Danielle was composing poems day and night. She carried untidy sheaves of paper with her everywhere and hoped that when their sentences were up, she and Victor could purchase a kit that would allow her to store her work on the threadlike tapes that one fed into the small holes below video screens. The people in the retirement units all carried spools of threads, the unvarying tales of their lives. Meantime, she had only the little recorder from which she transcribed her work onto old-fashioned sheets of paper.

It was less than a month from the conclusion of his sentence when Victor saw his daughter rush past the custard stand, her red Botticellian hair streaming behind her. He knew that she recognized him by the way she stared, averted her head, and walked faster. She ran. He shouted her name, accidentally triggering the vanilla spigot, which extruded a soft corrugated column of frozen custard that sagged to the ground, where it coiled upon itself. He pursued her, rushing down the stairs for the Uptime transport, where those who were allowed traveled home into the future, having come from there only to do their day's work. (Sometimes he had a vivid memory of the cell on Riker's Island, the car thief smoking an end-twisted, smuggled cigarette, talking from the bunk below, his voice rising with the sweet smoke. "Shit, man, there ain't nothin' in the future that's gonna help you. What you think, they gonna make it easy just because you said you did everything like they said you did, like a damn fool?") Wilma rushed into the transport, staring at him through the window, her face pale and troubled. Was it possible that she commuted from here to a time further into the future?

That evening, facing Danielle across the kitchen table, with Lanza's voice shaking the speaker of the old phonograph, he said he was afraid of going back to 1959.

"Our love is built on crime," Danielle said. "And art and literature."

"She's in the future," he said. "Wilma is in the future. I've got to go there. To see her. To talk with her."

"To do what?" Danielle asked. She plucked at her hair, crossed and uncrossed her legs, pinched her lips together. "I think it's too risky. I think it's like me going to see my mother."

They were both quiet. They realized that what they had together had never been tested by anyone or anything outside themselves. In their own times, it would have been family and friends. Meeting Victor, Danielle's mother would have grimaced, as she had at Danielle's trial, sitting just behind the expensive lawyer paid for by her sons. All Danielle had wanted, really, was to get away from her mother. To forget the redness that had spurted from Solly's throat, the limpness of his body that fell upon her like a huge bag of sugar. That night, as Victor groaned above her, she turned her face to the wall.

Twice more Victor saw his daughter. Each time, she rushed past, with two or three lines of people between herself and his outstretched hand. The third time, he threw himself into the crowd and seized her by both arms, his heart pounding, his face sticky with sweat, the smell of old cooking oil coming off his clothes.

"I don't know you," she said, staring him in the eyes.

He loosened his grasp as her gaze turned cold and her arms stiffened. He was sure it was Wilma. He released her, and she continued rushing with the crowd to the Uptime transport. That evening, Danielle begged him to give it up. "We don't even know what the city is really like," she said. "We don't know if all that news is propaganda. We don't know if the city is all rubble from some bomb. If there's a plague. If there's secret police everywhere. We don't know anything. What difference could it make if Wilma recognized you?"

Victor sat with his hands between his legs. "I just can't," he mumbled.

Two days later, he again followed Wilma to the Uptime transport, though he hid behind others. He could not discern any difference between it and the Downtime transport. Most of the passengers seemed fatigued from a day's work, and there were students looking dazed, and some people were whispering their poems or narratives into their recorders. The transport did seem faster than the Downtime one. He felt a buzzing in his body, a kind of whirring around his head, but he was not dizzy. Then the transport began to climb, and he realized they would be traveling above ground. But when they achieved what he knew must be street level, the windows of the transport seemed covered with aluminum foil. And when the doors opened at the first stop, passengers disembarked into a blinding white light. He saw a man like himself, shoulders rounded, and a white-haired woman with her hand on his arm. She could have been Ida, stooped from years of osteoporosis. They stepped off into the blinding light. They disappeared. Several stops later, Wilma got off and he was paralyzed with fear. What if this was not another future but a void, a holding tank, a quasi-nothingness?

Before he could move, the doors ballooned shut. He rode the rest of the way standing, clutching the center pole. Luckily, the transport reversed direction, and he got off at the 14th Street Station, convinced that he could not enter another time until his sentence was completed. It was the only explanation.

That evening, Danielle confessed to taking the Uptime transport. "I had to know," she said.

"What did you see?" he asked.

"The old neighborhood. It was like being on the Jerome Avenue line all over again. I saw the Mosholu Parkway stop. The brown beams on the Tudor apartment buildings. I saw where the Grand Concourse ended. The buildings with murals in the lobbies. I saw the hot-bagel shop under the El, and across from that the David Marcus Theater where I saw *Mondo Cane.* I saw the Temple on Gun Hill Road, near Montefiore Hospital. I thought I was coming home from the job I once had on Burnside Avenue. I began thinking what I would make for dinner, what my mother would eat."

Then she realized that her sentence had been up for almost forty-eight hours. "It must have been a leap year thing," she said. "I forgot that. They must have counted the leap year days somehow, so I got extra credit. I'm free, Victor!"

"But you were in the future?" he said.

"I didn't feel any difference," she said.

"Maybe," Victor said, "it wasn't the future. Maybe, with your sentence up, the future starts with where you left off. Maybe we can't skip over anything."

"Maybe it was a different past," she said. "Maybe they're giving us a chance to do something different."

Victor almost choked on the thought. If he went back, could he stop his wife from leaving him? Would he, this time, rage at Cosimo's paintings? He again followed Wilma onto the Uptime transport, trying to conceal himself among the few passengers. Through the clear windows, he saw the city he had once known, the old brick apartment buildings, the ragged backyards, Yankee Stadium, the Harlem River. He could smell the anisette biscuits baking at the Stella Doro plant on upper Broadway. He realized that Wilma was going home to Davidson Avenue, and he worried that he might look down and see his wife carrying bundles home from the A&P. Wilma got off at the old stop, and he watched her descend the stairs as the train pulled out. She looked as she did when taking night classes, her gait slow, her youthful face unnaturally drawn. He felt a pang of longing and began banging on the window, yelling her name. The few passengers ignored him. Had he, after all, ruined her life? He had such trouble breathing that he must have fainted. When he awoke, he was seated and riding in the opposite direction, the only passenger on the transport when it pulled into 14th Street.

Danielle was waiting for him. She had crammed her manuscripts into a large manila envelope. Her clothes, including some of Ida's underwear and scarves, were stuffed into an embroidered cloth bag with two wooden handles that snapped into each other. She had washed her hair and it shone in the gray fluorescence of the vapor tubes that lined the station. She smiled nervously. "I'm ready." She looked pale, slightly sunken, in spite of her prefulgent hair, like someone just released from prison. She threw her shoulders back. "I think," she said, "that we should go onto the Uptime transport together. I think that before we decide to stay here or go back, we should try to go further forward." "But then we'll have to be people who haven't lived yet. And whose stop should we get off at, yours or mine, the one for Davidson Avenue or Mosholu Parkway?" He was still unsteady from having followed his daughter to what had seemed the old time. Danielle looked frail but young. He tried not to hunch over. He was after all free. He loved Danielle's hair, her voice cracking like a jazz singer's in the middle of sentences, her eyes bright with unwritten poems and stories, her way of pinching his arm as she talked.

"Maybe we should go to your stop first," he said, "and then double-back to mine."

They took the Uptime transport, Danielle with her bulging envelope on her knees. Victor kept her carrying bag on his lap, trying not to be aware of Ida's things within. He had, in fact, begun to remember Ida. Her life on the Lower East Side of Manhattan, her parents' candy and newsstand like a kiosk built against the wall of the tenement they owned on 7th Street, off Avenue C. Around the corner was the luncheonette owned by his cousin Zina. It was while helping out at the luncheonette that he had met Ida, her voice breaking upon him like a wave of clear water.

"Do you mind?" Danielle asked. She wanted something from the bag and asked Victor to hold her envelope while she poked among Ida's and her own things.

Ida had expected him to own his own establishment, like her parents, like his cousin. Her sister would soon marry the son of the man who owned the little kosher restaurant that sold franks and knishes on the other side of 7th Street, opposite her parents' kiosk. Ida was quite prepared to be the energetic woman behind a counter. But it had seemed such an improvement, after she married Victor, to move to the Bronx, to have trees on one's street. His job with ABC Concessions was supposed to be temporary. With cash gifts from his uncles and cousins (nothing from his brother who'd gone into debt for his own deli) and her parents, he was supposed to become somebody. She never expected him to return money to men who lost their teaching jobs because they were once Communists. ("We can't keep this," Victor had said. "What did they do wrong cursing poverty?") She didn't know what a fellow traveler was. He'd never expected to lose what was left in a scheme to control all the roast chestnut and frankfurter stands west of 7th Avenue. His fortunes went down. Ida's weight went up. Wilma became a difficult and moody child. It was only now, as the transport rode smoothly up above ground, past the Bronx Terminal Market, and with Danielle quietly recording a new poem, that he remembered the young Ida, before her upper arms sagged and her voice became scratchy from cigarettes. There had always been something fistlike in her nature. How had it become a grasp around his throat? What hair she had! In the morning it was like autumn leaves on fire.

Danielle tittered at something she was saying into the flat, flexible recorder. Her elbows dug into the carrying bag on her lap. Victor studied the bony line of her jaw, the slight tremble of her head whenever she spoke with feeling, as she did now. Was she remembering her mother? What if he had to meet that woman? What if this was not the future at all? He remembered his daughter coming home from classes, after Ida had left for good. He had tried to cook a meal. Poking at the runny eggs, she'd said, "I know you mean well. But I really don't like this."

Then he saw her. His daughter entered the car through the lips of the soft black rubber gasket that separated one car of the transport from another. She carried a college spiral notebook and a thick book on the history of modern art and had dark circles around her eyes.

He stood up, and Danielle's envelope slipped from his lap onto the floor. "Wilma, it's me!"

She looked at him and grimaced and hurried through the gasket at the other end of the car. He watched the hem of her dress slip through and disappear. He looked out the windows and down. There on the street was Ida pulling a shopping cart with several bags of groceries from the A&P. The transport was pulling into his old stop. He looked at Danielle whispering into her recorder.

"I can't!" he yelled. "I just can't! God forgive me!"

Danielle looked startled, but before she could say a word, he dashed through the open doors out onto the platform, his shoes clomping loudly.

He raced downstairs to the level of the token booth, where a man was half-asleep. He saw his daughter ahead of him, descending the stairs to street level. He called but she ignored him. And as he followed her to the stone stairs that led up to Davidson Avenue, he realized that she could not hear him. His appeals made no more impression on her than the slightly sour odor wafting from the closed coffee shop in the little alleyway that ended at the stairs. Inside the apartment house, while his daughter took the elevator, and while he heard the deep hum of the departing transport that was taking Danielle further uptown to Mosholu Parkway and a life without him, he went up the stained staircase.

He walked through the closed door of the apartment. Ida was saying to Eve, "If it's Lou's in Ventnor, maybe it's something Victor can help with." Solly was leaning against a kitchen cabinet, frowning. Eve was about to say, "What? Like the chestnuts? We don't need to lose everything." Victor himself cut in, as if he'd never left. "No," he said. "We're not interested. I have an idea for something in the fast-food line." He looked at his sister-in-law and said, "Not chestnuts, either." Solly shrugged and looked relieved. "Well . . ." Eve said. "Also," Victor said, turning to his brother-in-law, "we won't need any cold cuts!" Solly was bewildered. "Listen," Ida began, "I . . ." "Besides," Victor said, "Wilma wants to go to art school, and we want to help her. We can't afford Ventnor."

At that very moment, Wilma entered the apartment with a thin young man who was wearing a black topcoat. ("He looked like Hamlet," Ida would say years later. "No sybarite.") Wilma kissed her aunt and uncle on the cheek, avoiding her uncle's lingering hand, and said, "Mama, Papa, I want you to meet Cosimo." The young man with dark unruly hair and sunken cheeks clicked his heels and bowed. "We're in the same drawing class," Wilma said. "Look." She held up a charcoal sketch of Cosimo. He was nude, seated on a bar stool, his penis shaped like a little finger, his gaze turned to a romantic distance that must have been merely the back of the classroom and the disorder of a supplies table.

"My God!" Ida said. "Is this what you do in school?"

She looked sternly at Cosimo, who nodded, and said, "It's really not a bad likeness."

Wilma laughed.

Later that evening, Ida, with the shopping cart unpacked, was seated at the kitchen table, sipping a cup of tea, a cigarette smoldering in an ashtray, her hair pulled neatly back in a more businesslike version of the same hair her daughter wore in a ponytail. She had handsome lines around her mouth, her girth and upper arms as Victor remembered them before she dieted. Though tired, she seemed in the twilight mood that follows successful labor. After her sister and Solly had departed, and Wilma gone off somewhere with Cosimo, she had told him there were things they'd need, if they weren't going off on a vacation. It hadn't seemed an accusation, like the other time, when Wilma had come home by herself, tired, with books under her arm, and later Ida had turned away from him in bed.

She stood up and approached him. He held his breath, not certain even now that she could see him.

"Solly didn't talk nice to you." She took his hand and placed it on her breast and pinched him on the cheek. The odor of Parliaments came off her hair. Down the hill, on Jerome Avenue, the El shook and chattered as the downtown train squealed into the station.

"Some things you can't do anything about," he replied, and shrugged.

COURTSHIP

1964

Boots told Lucille on the phone that it was about time. And she complained about her own husband, his hours managing the Woolworth's on Steinway Street, his eyeing the girls. She talked about

(1) her sister Mary's marriage to a retired army sergeant, a terrible infection that ate away half his jaw,
(2) her two daughters,
(3) the bombing of the travel agency on Broadway by Croatian terrorists,
(4) the stiffness in the legs of her dog Gypsy.

"And don't give in when he begs you to come back. What a mistake! What a mistake!"

Lucille, in a glass-doored phone booth on a corner of the Mobil station on 31st Street in Astoria, nodded as if she were seated opposite her friend. She hung up just before the elevated train thundered overhead. Her swept-up dyed red hair and ample middle-aged body attracted the stares of two mechanics smoking near the gas pumps. She had told Boots she'd moved out, without describing the furnished room's wooden bed with nicked posts, the soft cavity of the mattress, the smeared mirror, the news on someone's radio coming through the wall.

Fifty dollars a week. She wondered what it would be like in her
new job at Hanlon's, not being a customer, and waiting on her
friends, Boots and Adelaide and Annie.

She went back up to the room in the frame house where the
upper floor was shared with a man with respiratory difficulties
and, she was told, a young woman. There was a linen closet
and one bathroom. Quilted needlework in frames hung on the
walls. "Welcome to Our Home."

No, she thought. She hadn't left Joe just because their son,
Robbie, was out of the house. She doused herself with perfume, went down the stairs and out the common entrance that
let onto a wide porch. There was another small flight of stairs,
then a little walkway cut through grass and led to a gate in the
wire-mesh fence and the sidewalk. It would be difficult to get
in and out and not be observed by the landlady, a woman who
sank her hands into the pockets of her housedress, while her
husband drank beer and watched TV, when he wasn't scolding
the children.

Later, seated on the barstool in Hanlon's, Lucille continued
to think how easy it was to be observed, and crossed her legs,
swinging the top one, but stopped when she realized that was
her sister's habit.

"You'll have plenty to do soon," Hanlon said. A widower
with flushed, jowled face, he was a parody of the retired policeman, gruff, garrulous, doubtful of the goodness in man. He
had in fact hurt his back in the IRT tunnel between the 14th
and 23rd Street stations and retired on disability from the
Transit Workers Union.

She didn't tell him about leaving Joe. And she declined
Anthony's offer of dinner, the cook, Anthony, with deep hollows around his eyes, who inhabited the kitchen like a lair.

A few workers from the plant around the corner came in for beers, and left, giving her a nod, the quiet broken by Hanlon clinking and arranging bottles, while she told herself again that she wasn't leaving just because her son, Robbie, was gone. Robbie. Swaggering. Small. Looking like Joe with his hard-muscled jaw and the hands that never made a wasted motion. A wild look in his eyes. His hair already thin.

The steady fizzle of the beer sign in the window got on her nerves the way the buzzing of her kitchen clock did when she was not working in one of the stores on Steinway Street to pick up money for drapes or an end table—things Joe would not pay for.

Hanlon reached into the cooler and pulled out a container of milk.

"You got an ulcer?"

"Not me." He drank the milk slowly, smacked his lips. "Ah."

(5) Joe in his shorts. A hot night. His legs thin and hairy: he lifts the container of milk to his lips, the light from the open refrigerator illuminating his Adam's apple bobbing in the muscular throat. She tells him to use a glass. He waves her away with his free hand. She tells him she wants a new rug for the living room. He stops drinking. He stands before the shelves of leftovers, enjoying cool emanations. He shakes his head, jaw muscles clenching. "You want it, you get the money for it." "You sonuvabitch." "It's like livin' in a furniture store here." "You love it." "Yeah," he says, closing the refrigerator, entering the kitchen, small in his shorts, his torso white and boyish. He sits down and says nothing. "Robbie's quit his job," she says. He brings his hand slowly to his brow and wipes his palm back over his bald head. He rubs his hands together

and she remembers the freak case of mumps, his swollen testi-
cles. Now he is like someone rotating a stick to make fire.
"Well?" He sucks at his teeth. "Again," he says. And she feels
heavy, slow, listening to him suck at his teeth.

Hanlon wiped his mouth with the end of his apron.

"How's Laurie?"

Hanlon explained his daughter's doctor said she had to stop
having them so fast.

"Oh, I don't know. These small ones have alot of kids and
they still keep their looks. My sister was like that. Even now,
one kid drunk, the other crazy, she keeps her looks." A nervous
wreck.

(6) Robbie's phone calls. Trouble with his back. Fell down
during calisthenics. Hospital. Nothing wrong, they said.
Spasms, Mom. In the head. She told him to come home and he
said that was stupid. He was no kid. There was a war starting
in Southeast Asia. She cried. He said, you know what you're
doing to me? He wrote an angry letter, then he called to
apologize, and she was cold, and he said she always sounded so
dead on the phone. What was wrong? He couldn't concentrate.
Had an accident, doing carpentry, building a platform. Lost
the tip of his middle finger to a circular saw.

She slid off the bar stool and tied on the apron that would
protect her skirt. "You tell Laurie if she has any more kids she's
crazy."

Boots, Adelaide, Annie sat at the round table nearest the
bar, leaning on the checkerboard tablecloth, rolling their eyes
when Lucille served young men. They told her she looked
great. Great. Adelaide still talked about her good-looking husband who had left so long ago. Boots said he probably had

died. Adelaide shuddered, her narrow face like Bette Davis's after a stroke, made wide with applications of blush, black hair glossy and dyed, her small voice scratchy from cigarettes. "I hope not!"

"You're as bad as I am," Annie said, squeezing Adelaide's arm. "That's the way I thought about Lou. I still think about him that way." Annie looked about the room, dark-blonde hair touching her shoulders, jeans snug on long legs, her straight white teeth and high-pitched voice too girlish for Boots, who chided her. "What's next. Pimples?" But Annie was the most independent. The most educated. She and Lou had run a gift shop in the Village. They'd had a camp in the Adirondacks. They'd done everything right. And still divorced.

"Have a seat. Come on." Boots waved to Lucille, who'd just returned dishes to the kitchen, where Anthony, the cook, had earlier been joking, his stutter making him almost equine as his upper lip curled back from his teeth, eyelids half lowered, the trapped word gathering everything to itself, until giving it up he would simply laugh. Loudly.

"If they need something, they'll call you," Boots said. She nodded toward the young couple hunched over their white wine. "Take a load off." Lucille sat and exhaled loudly. "My feet. God." "Listen, you're doing great. Great." Boots began to rub her friend's back. "Oh, you are." Annie leaned over and kissed her cheek. Lucille accepted a cigarette. "My feet. They're burning up." She reached down and touched a puffiness in her ankles she hadn't seen since the incident at Annie's cabin. After she'd fought with Joe.

(7) He saying, "What. What's going on?" coming to get her out of Hanlon's where she'd been all night. Sitting in the car with her. "Listen." His bald head damp. He removed his

glasses and wiped them with a handkerchief that smelled of detergent. This calmness as if she were an irate customer at his gas station, this mock sympathy for someone angry over excessive charges. Because the car was still not fixed. Neither was she. Not fixed. Not anything. Not sober. "I'm tired. Just tired." "You want a drink or what." He waved toward the pint in his glove compartment. "Tea," she said. And later, in the car, after he went to the diner and brought back tea so hot that she burned the roof of her mouth, he rolled down the steamed-up window. Did she have a boyfriend? Was it money? The tea was awful. From the bottle he kept in the glove compartment he poured bourbon into a paper cup. Quaffed it. Who would guess? she said. You can't do this, he said. He was bleary, telling her, she could see, that the bill was correct.

(8) The fault was in the car. In her.

He leaned against her suddenly, tried to kiss her, but she turned her head away. She heard him catch his breath. He removed his glasses again, rubbed his eyes, leaning forward so that she saw his damp, tired face.

(9) Overhead, the moon slipped behind clouds.

"Oh, let me get it." Annie restrained Lucille, who had started to rise when the couple motioned for their check. Annie brought the check to the table. She brought the money to Hanlon, who winked at Lucille, and Annie deposited the dollar tip in front of her. "There."

Lucille touched her ankle again. Annie said, "You ought to put your feet up." The last time her ankles had swelled, Lucille had died in the emergency room. Anaphylactic shock. Yellow jackets swarmed out of the ground she had been stamping on. She was rushed to the hospital, her whole body bloated. And for a second or two, no vital signs on that stainless steel table.

Nothing. Blackness. Nothing at all. Because of a duck. A merganser. A fuzzy-headed, brown-tufted merganser that had lost its right leg to a snapping turtle. Hopping up the slope after her. She'd been tossing bread crumbs into the pond, Annie's pond. All the talk of Lou and Joe. And Robbie. Even here, with August chill, the loud droning of seaplanes taking campers to remote islands, the lumber yard now visible, its squawking PA audible since the logging road had been cut through the woods, past Annie's two-room A-frame. Even here. The merganser hopping up the slope, quacking, demanding. Lucille slipping in the soft ground carpeted by brown pine needles, holding onto trees. Smooth, latex-like lichens breaking off in her hands. That creature insisting on being fed. Cared for. Until she turned, near the grill set into bricks, stamping her feet, shrieking, go away! Go away! And the yellow jackets burst from a hole, her legs, arms, face alive with pinpoint stings entering her like the tips of hot wires.

"It's for you." Hanlon held the phone out.

For the next several weeks Joe courted her. She had Wednesday and Sunday off, and he got home early enough to call for her, flowers in hand, the landlady's husband snickering as he watched Joe come through the gate and along the walkway and up the stairs onto the porch. Sometimes Joe brought costume jewelry, and though she knew he'd purchased it from one of the types who came through his gas station and also sold condoms by the dozen, she didn't mind. She had a second hole pierced in her right ear by Annie, above her lobe, in the fleshy part of the helix, and bought little garnet and sapphire earrings, one of which she wore in the new hole, while in her lobes hung golden hoops or little triangles that poked Joe when she gave him

tantalizing kisses on the mouth. But she refused to go to a
motel with him. They ate in the Oyster Bay restaurant, went to
Radio City Music Hall, rode the Staten Island Ferry. Once he
took her to Mamma Leone's for the green pasta she loved. She
let him feel her up in the car; and on the porch, just outside the
front door,

(10) she stroked his penis through his pants.

"So you won't forget me."

But she wouldn't go all the way. He told her he was having
wet dreams, and sometimes, working on a car, he got sudden
erections.

Early each evening, she walked the several blocks to Hanlon's. Parking spaces on the street were filled by Dodges and
Chevrolets, with here and there a car pulled up to a hydrant, its
parking lights on, the small brick apartment buildings all
showing lit windows. Tiled courtyards built in the Thirties
echoed with the shrill voices of children. People were returning
home, walking from the IND subway stop on Steinway Street
or from the elevated BMT stop at Broadway, and she thought
how lucky she was that she didn't need public transportation.

She wrote Robbie, telling him about the job.

She didn't mention moving out, so Joe had to bring Robbie's letters when they met for a date.

(11) She didn't tell Joe that Anthony the cook gave her
funny little books of stories to read or that his dark eyes and
smooth face and baritone voice were nice.

When he wasn't stammering.

Boots got birthday theater tickets from one of her daughters
and took Lucille along. They talked about their friend Irene
whose son at the age of ten was working with an agency that

did TV commercials. Irene was stashing it away. Lucille said it wasn't so good, raising a son in show business. "Those kids are all screwed up." Sometimes she and her sister and Boots would sit in Boots' kitchen drinking tea,

    (12) munching raw vegetables,
          talking about their children.

And the sisters Amelia and Elizabeth. Adelaide always defended Elizabeth who, she insisted, had physical problems. And lousy doctors. Lucille's sister and Boots both said Lucille oughtn't to sleep with Joe. "What for? Let him get blue balls," Boots said. "Oh, I don't know," the sister said, "he's really trying, you don't want him to stop that. But once you open the store."

"Jesus," she said. Her entry into the apartment was a shock. The furniture she'd picked, the drapes she'd hung, the lamps and rugs she'd scrimped for were things belonging to a person she had forgotten. When Joe asked her to sit down in the kitchen, with Chee-Chee the parakeet sidling up to the bars of his cage, ready for combat, she said, "I don't like it here anymore."

"It's yours as much as mine." His wave encompassed the entire apartment.

"It's just yours."

"Come on, sit down."

She sat on the edge of the chair, her back stiff, her red hair vivid from a recent dye job swept up in a flaming mass, her perfume filling the kitchen.

"At least take off your coat," he said.

She looked up. "Not for long."

"Just one drink. One drink."

"Everything looks so clean," she said.

At the bar in the living room, he poured two drinks. "No one's ever here." She winced momentarily. What stopped him from bringing other women? He sat opposite her, by the window where she used to sit, under the philodendron suspended from the ceiling. "Cheers," he said, and clinked the glass she hadn't picked up yet.

She slipped out of her coat and raised her drink, peering over the top of the glass. She tried to smile, but a wave of exhaustion swept over her. They'd had a pleasant evening, eating in the Oyster Bay, listening to the live piano, but their talk had been tinged with boredom. She watched Joe fidget, running his finger along the edge of the table, his eyes tense and enlarged behind his glassses, his half-smile.

"Robbie called last night," he said.

"Oh?"

"I didn't want to tell you before. He's okay, there's nothing wrong. I didn't mention it before." He shrugged.

"And?"

"I told him you wanted to be on your own for a while." He looked away.

"What d'you mean, 'for a while'?"

"Look," he said.

"You had no right to tell him. It's my business."

"Working in a bar, for chrissake."

"It's my fucking business!"

"You got that right." His face pinched into a scornful mask.

"What? You got something to say?"

(1) She told him she didn't need anymore of his little love-
       ins.

(2)   He wiped his hand over the back of his head, saying he
      didn't need this, all day killing himself, while she sat
      and complained.
(3)   She reminded him she wasn't here at all.
(4)   She didn't know why she'd come.
(5)   He said she was his wife.
"Since when!"
(6)   He told her to sit down.
(7)   At least she was alive, she said. Not a zombie.
(8)   What about Robbie?
(9)   He had no business, Joe, to say anything.
(10) He wanted to know who it was. Just who. That's all.
      Who she was sleeping with.
(11) Oh, she said, I fuck for anyone. Anyone with balls.
From his sitting position, where he was crouched over his
drink, he clenched his fingers into a fist and punched her in the
abdomen. She gasped, doubled over, tried to catch her breath.
He held his head in his hands. He removed his glasses. Jesus
Christ! He looked at her, as she sucked asthmatically for air.
She began to pant. Breathe slower, he said. You'll hyperventi-
late. He reached for one of the paper bags in the cabinet next to
the sink. Here, breathe into this. She waved him off. She
remembered the respirator tube inserted in her mouth in the
Adirondack emergency room. The way he came for her.
  She took the glass of water. After three sips, she poured it
into the sink.
(12) "I'll walk home," she said.

"You got your own life," Boots said, leaning forward on her
heavy arms.
  "Some day," Lucille said.

It was no good, what others told you. And twice now, she had dreamt of her mother. Illness not in evidence on her smooth face, white hair forming a cloudy background to hazel eyes that had lost their watery look, her mother sat at the old porcelain kitchen table, pulling out the silverware drawer, rummaging among knives, forks, spoons, though what she withdrew was a rubber band. "Look at all that shit!" Her mother had never used such language. That table Lucille had given away when her mother died, watched them load it into the Salvation Army truck, along with the steamer trunk that smelled of an old woman.

"God." She awoke abruptly. Furniture. If she got her own apartment, she'd need furniture.

Three days later she found a letter from Robbie left by Joe at the rooming house.

(1a) He couldn't believe it.
(2a) He didn't know things had been so bad.
(3a) He blamed his father's long hours.
(4a) He blamed her for not doing more with herself.
(5a) He blamed the apartment for being too small.
(6a) He blamed her sister and Boots and Irene and Annie
        and Adelaide. All those women.
(7a) He blamed television.
(8a) He blamed Hanlon's.
(9a, 10a, 11a, 12a) He blamed himself.

She avoided Boots without knowing why. Their friend Irene was dating a widowered postman named Happy, and when she wasn't burbling about him, she was showing Lucille the model agency's photos of her son dressed in a baseball uniform or eating huge cupcakes. In the diner on Steinway Street, Lucille listened to her sister, who smoked cigarette after cigarette, pumping one leg atop the other, keeping time to the quick music of her pulse, detailing how the men had carried her husband up the stairs, his bleeding ulcer bringing him to death's door.

Twice Lucille visited Annie and her two German shepherds, Hillary and Fyodor. Annie dated younger men. Whatever had gone wrong with her marriage, Annie had dismissed it as her husband's problem with her love of things natural, her zest, a word she used as often as *joie*. "You know, men expect us to give them their feelings about life. As if we were little machines they could attach themselves to, after they've been chopping wood or closing a business deal. And if we do anything on our own, right away it's phallic. As if we were castrating them. What a bore." She didn't have that problem with younger men.

Often Lucille awoke twisted in her blanket. She remembered the nights Joe came home exhausted, refusing food, drinking until he fell asleep at the kitchen table, leaving her to sleep alone. Or she'd lead him to the bathroom, take him to bed. Cover him. She could hear the man in the next room breathing stertorously through the sheet-rock wall the landlady's husband had erected, dividing the former living room of an upstairs apartment into two rentable quarters. Further down the hall was the other room, where a thin young woman with bad complexion tried secretly to cook on a hot plate, until the landlady came up and vociferously forbad it. They all took clean linens from the hall closet. Lucille wondered why she and Joe had never bought a house. How she herself would manage, with only the salary from Hanlon's. What if she became ill? Her work experience always marginal, selling drapes or working in dress stores. Once, thanks to Adelaide, helping their friend Amelia in the paint store, when Amelia was visiting her sister Elizabeth in Creedmoor. Everything temporary. And when the Christmas rush was over, or workers had returned from vacation, she was back to zero. In the kitchen. Calling Boots. But she'd never thought about

(1) traipsing back and forth,

(2) nine-to-five,

(3) actually six to eleven-thirty, with Sunday off,

(4) squeezing in her shopping on days when everything was crowded.

Well. This was temporary. The room. She needed her own apartment, furniture, her name over the bell downstairs. In the mailbox

(5) a divorce.

Anthony, the cook, gave her books she couldn't make sense of. She met him to see a foreign film in Manhattan, something German, depressing. She sat with Anthony in a coffee shop, while he talked about society's madness for money, the developing war, his eyes flashing, his stutter sometimes producing a wetness around the mouth, sensuous and repellent. He was a writer. He'd published a story in a small magazine in New Orleans. He gave her two of his stories to read. She enjoyed the one about the old-maid aunt dancing furiously at her niece's wedding. The other, about a young man in prison, smoking, staring at the barred window, while being interrogated by a man who looked like Hanlon, was confusing. His crime had something to do with a woman. But Anthony was interested in her, and in Hanlon's kitchen their bodies touched and she remembered the feel of him when she tried to sleep at night. They went to the movies again, and she let him fondle her in the dark, oddly moaning, though she wasn't that aroused. She wondered why she did that.

After work one night, after she'd stripped off her panty hose with great relief, Anthony invited her to his apartment. They walked down a driveway between two four-family houses. Around back, to the left, was the private entrance into a basement, where the owner, an old Armenian tailor now retired, a widower, had erected partitions, installed a stove, added an old refrigerator with an ice-cube compartment that caked with frost. The toilet was in an alcove just outside the apartment, next to a shower stall. It was all, Lucille thought, just a cellar. She felt lucky having the room she did. Anthony became foolish, wiggling his eyebrows, saying, "Well? Well?" sweeping his hand before him, taking deep bows. She didn't want to sit at the little table which, with three chairs, served as the kitchen at the end of the room, near the door. Down the other end was a mattress on a box spring, cartons of books, many on psychic phenomena, a typewriter on top of an old-fashioned trunk that Anthony used as his desk.

"Is that where you work?" She asked if they could sit there, so Anthony brought over one of the kitchen chairs. He offered her the deeply cushioned swivel chair he used when typing. When she demurred, saying it was his chair, she couldn't use it, he slid his hand up and down her back, saying, make yourself at home. She laughed. He went to the other end of the room and returned with a bottle of cheap brandy. He winked. And she began to drink with abandon.

All she remembered later was him leaning over her, telling her to get up. Could she get up? He was agitated. Could she get up? She felt sick to her stomach. A terrible headache. Whether he had been sipping his drinks while she swallowed all of hers she didn't know. Before she passed out, she remembered him laughing. A lot. Loudly.

And now, walking down Broadway where she couldn't find a cab, though Anthony had offered to accompany her home,

asking, "Are you sure? Are you sure?" when she told him she
was fine—now she could feel

(6) his semen oozing out of her,

(7) a wetness moving down her thighs.

She could say she was raped. She'd tell Boots she'd been
raped.

The next afternoon, she found another letter from Robbie
that Joe had left. She remembered the whine in Robbie's voice,
the look in his eyes from childhood, when she took him to the
doctor and he sulked and wouldn't let her touch him. She
thought more about getting her own apartment, scraping together the security deposit, paying an agent. She could die in
such a place and not be discovered for days. "Unidentified
woman found . . ." She shivered. Afraid. Of what?

Thursday evening, she was cold to everyone. She had found a
note from Joe at the rooming house. Robbie had called. She
didn't realize how angry she was until Anthony tried to touch
her in the kitchen. "Hands off, hands off! I know what you did,
you creep. I know!" He avoided her when she came in with
dishes and scraped the leavings into the can. She watched his
knuckles whiten as he squeezed a rag over the sink.

At ten o'clock, Hanlon told her she could go, and she
stepped out into the cloudy night. A few drops were beginning
to fall. When she looked across the street, and saw Joe's car,
she knew she had expected it to be there. He walked toward
her, limping with fatigue, dressed in clean work clothes. His
face was gray and his slight swagger unconvincing as he
stopped to hike up his pants.

"This is crazy," he said.

"Maybe I'm crazy," she said.

He kept a distance between them. "I can't stand this."

"What," she said flatly.

"This." He waved his hand. He looked so small. Tired. "You shouldn't be here."

"Just tell me what's going on. You got a boyfriend. Or what?"

It wasn't that he wanted her, he just didn't want being alone. The clock's *buzz, click, buzz.* Robbie's complaints. The smell of emptiness that drifted from the dusty drapes, the unwashed sheets, the sticky shot glasses, the milky birdshit in Chee-Chee's cage. The long stairwell mixing in its odors of spiced ham and smoked sausage that still clung to the walls from Merkel's Pork Store downstairs that had moved years ago. One could buy gyros, souvlaki, salads with bitter olives, the ex-pork store now a sandwich shop set into the building and adjoining the entryway that led to two apartments, the top one where she had lived for two decades.

"We can move," he said. "Whatever you want. Jackson Heights."

"Yeah. All you need is a nice little wife with a nice little tush."

"What?"

"Forget it! Just forget it! Leave me alone!" She started to walk away.

Anthony stepped out of Hanlon's, into the street, spatula in hand. "Hey," he said, lifting his chin and jerking the shiny implement toward Joe. "Hey." Lucille could see his upper lip tremble as words piled up behind his teeth. Later, she remembered cursing. Someone touching her. A pair of hands tearing at her dress. One knee driving itself between her legs. But the howls were hers. And it was she who snatched the spatula out of Anthony's hand and whipped it across Joe's cheek, the sound like slapped meat, a perfect red rectangle appearing in front of Joe's ear, his lip cut, glasses knocked awry. "You did it now," he said. "You really did it." He shook his head.

She threw the spatula across the street and stormed down 34th Avenue.

Back at the room, she lay in bed fully clothed. She felt as if someone had walked out of her body and left it for the landlady to find in the morning, when it began to stink.

(8)   She'd be an old woman with cats.

(9)   Her legs spindly in the calves.

(10) Her upper arms huge and flabby.

(11) She'd need help to mount the stairs of the Broadway bus.

(12) Every Saturday morning, Robbie, a half-bald veteran, out of work, would sit in her kitchen that smelled of unwashed clothes. He'd be eating buttered bread, drinking tea with condensed milk and sugar, whining about the supermarket that fired him.

I'll be my mother, she thought.

Let him suffer.

She leaped out of bed.

Walking back up 34th Avenue, she felt damp and malodorous. The dress clung to her body. She passed Hanlon's on the opposite side of the street and could see Hanlon wiping the bar, his face puffed. Anthony was gone. Hanlon leaned over the bar, his head down, his wild hair flattened as if he'd run into a wall, and she knew that's how he'd look over her, his huge belly pressing her down, the flabby white skin of his back bunched in her hands.

She walked crosstown, toward Broadway, past Precious Blood Church and Quinn's Funeral Home, the night air soothing her body, a cool relief swirling up her dress. Her scalp felt damp, her hair long, red, ravaged. She walked quickly, obsessively.

Suddenly, she was there, without knowing how she'd arrived. Standing across the street from the Gyros shop, she stared up at the bedroom windows of her old apartment. His. A sudden image of their bed. The driftwood from Jones Beach. Little Robbie waking her up one morning. Joe laughing.

Damn fool.

A car stopped for the red light. The man looked. Winked. Rolled his eyes. "Quack-quack-quack," she said, flapping her arms. He shrugged. The light turned green, and he gave her a last look before driving off.

What was Joe doing up there? The faint light on the shades had to be coming from further back in the apartment. He must be in the kitchen.

She reached in her purse for the crushed pack of cigarettes that had been there for over a week untouched. The cigarettes were broken up but the smell of the loose tobacco was pleasant. She lit a stub. How long since she'd eaten? Her body felt so empty. She yelled up at the window. "Hey! You!"

Nothing.

She exhaled. Tired. Her skin damp, releasing an odor. She was stranded there, in front of the old store, remembering hams hanging in the window. She laughed. It could happen. Carrying a sausage on the subway, riding back and forth from Astoria to Coney Island, standing in the train, shrieking at strangers, wielding the sausage. Another crazy lady.

She crossed the street. In the vestibule, she stared at his name in the mailbox. The other mailbox was blank, and she remembered him telling her the Bilottis had moved and now he was alone in the building. Just him and the sandwich shop. She climbed the narrow stairs. Each creak, each scratch

on the banister, even the old linoleum smell on the first landing as she passed the Bilotti apartment: she knew them all
before they happened. Out of breath, she reached the third
floor and looked up at the skylight that had shed a gray light
for so many years.

She heard the toilet flush, and waited, breathing hard, staring at the door. No voices. She knocked, and noticed how
yellowish her hands had become. The brown spots.

"Oh," he said. Without his glasses, he squinted at her. He
seemed removed, tired, standing in his shorts, and he looked
past her, down the stairs, then into her face. The red patch on
his cheek had risen like a pastry.

She waited.

He left the door open, and walked, slightly hunched, into
the kitchen.

(1) She saw how thin his legs were, his baggy shorts.

She waited in the hall.

(2) She watched him sit at the table, a shot-glass half raised,
his windburned head and neck strangely appended to his
white torso.

She walked in.

(3) With his back to her, he lifted the glass high, in a kind
of salute.

"No," she said.

(4) In the cramped corridor that led from the hallway to the
kitchen, she squeezed past the refrigerator and could
smell her body again. If she drank with him, it would
be . . .

He downed his drink and coughed.

(5) "Shit," he said. "Excuse me."

(6) "Sure."

She noticed the cover was over the parakeet's cage.

He turned and faced her.

(7) "You wanna sit?"

She shrugged, looking down on him.

(8) "I don't know."

(9) "Sit down at least!" His voice turned angry but he stopped.

She sat down opposite him.

(10) "God!"

(11) "Can't eat," he said, as if she'd asked him.

He poured another shot. His face and neck darkened in color. His body was so white, ghastly white.

She could see the boy in him. His habit of lounging in his shorts, that and his smallness, and now the eyes, the look of someone ashamed.

(12) "I'm sorry," she said.

"Doesn't matter," he said. "Don't upset yourself."

"I'm not upset!"

"Whatever." He waved his hand.

She sighed. Her feelings could still erupt.

"We're too old for this," he said, and looked away. "I don't know."

"Listen, I only wanted . . ." She trailed off.

He was looking up, and quickened, but when she stopped herself, he nodded and looked away. "I know," he said.

"Christ!" A self-hate swept over her. It was him, it was coming from him. "Oh, stop it," she said, "stop it, stop it."

"What do you want? What do you want from me?" He leaned over the table, facing her, the cords of his neck straining, discrete as thin fingers.

"Stop it!"

He sank back in his chair, rubbed his stomach, looked down at it, as if something had fallen into his navel.

Her sudden passion faded. She felt tired now. The mark on his cheek confronted her like a brand.

"I'm glad you're here."

"I know," she said.

He got up to touch her.

"Oh, no," she said. "Forget it."

He shrugged.

"Just never mind that!"

(1)   He walked over to the refrigerator, and standing before its open door, gulped milk from the container. He returned the container and grunted.

(2)   "What?" she said.

(3)   "Nothing."

(4)   "You were thinking something. What?"

(5)   "Forget it. Just forget it."

He sat down and poured himself another shot.

She felt dead. She couldn't move.

He finished his drink and grimaced.

(6)   "Agh."

(7)   "Well," she said.

The clock buzzed on the wall, and she felt the second hand sweep over her like a wand. She yawned.

(8)   "What are you gonna do?" he said, scowling.

(9)   "Yeah, what."

She began to slump in the chair.

(10)   "You can stay, if you want to." He looked away.

(11)   "I know," she said.

(12)   "It's up to you."

"Yeah." She felt a momentary bitterness. Why was it her choice? She was tired.

"You can have the bed. I'll sleep in Robbie's room."

She laughed. "You will? Really?" She laughed again.

"Forget it," he said.

(1)   "I'm sorry," she said, wiping her eyes.

(2)   "Make up your mind," he said.

He poured another drink.

(3)   "One last one," he said.

She waited. Then suddenly,

(4)   "Me too."

Behind her, a muffled cheep and scratching in Chee-Chee's cage. They each downed a shot. They looked at each other, trying to smile. It was something, she thought, her mother might have counseled.

(5)   Never hurts to smile.

(6)   All that crap.

Joe's glazed eyes gradually shifted their focus to the dripping faucet across the room. He turned to study the *plip-plip* and presented his good cheek to her. She remembered

(7)   breathing in the emergency room in the Adirondacks,

(8)   that tube taped into her mouth,

(9)   her throat sore,

(10) her eyes hurting,

(11) her entire body swollen,

        wondering if Robbie would know how she died.

Well. She was alive. She could actually hear the traffic control box on the corner of Broadway and 33rd clittering, lights turning green and yellow and red and green for an empty street.

(12) Clouds were sliding overhead, as she brushed the philodendron aside and looked out the rear window up at the moon.

$\mathscr{T}$HE TIP

1964

The weather had changed. From his bed he could see the sun slanting down through the window. He pulled himself up. With the dampness gone, the pains had stopped. As he stood, bracing himself by leaning on a chair and the bureau, the bed squeaked and a spring let go with a metallic snap. His wife turned over in her bed, and brushed back the stringy hair that clung to her forehead like wet roots. "It is time?" she asked. "Ya, ya. Go back to sleep. I see you before I go." He could smell her bed, the stale clothes, the bedpan, and looking at her he felt a dull tiredness as if he hadn't slept. He lowered himself into the chair, and rubbed the stump of his right leg that was gone above the knee. After changing into his underwear—his T-shirt gray inside the collar from the grease that never came out, either from the shirt or the creases in his neck—he pulled on his false leg, inserting his stump into the tubular opening and pushing it against the padding. He pulled the braces up over his shoulder, then finished dressing and lunged forward into the kitchen.

He was big, his gray hair sparse, inching up like stubble, his ears hunky, jutting stiffly from his head. It was Sunday, his turn to open the gas station, and he wore his baggy work pants and the denim jacket, the breast pocket of which sprouted three cigars.

On and off, thirty years he worked for Joe Mistrulli, he thought. Almost half his life that had begun in Krk, an island off the Croatian coast, opposite the Istrian peninsula. The olive trees hadn't died yet. His father drew their water from the wells. At the beach he caught octopus with his bare hands, and the tentacles reached up sometimes and sucked poisonously at his arm. He worked fast. Later, in Pennsylvania, he lost his leg in the quarry. The big rocks, the drills banging, the big crane. When that chain snapped, it was the rocks came alive and took something back. Eye for an eye. But at least, working in the bakery in New York, he learned English. He couldn't be on the tug boats with the other Yugos, not with his leg that way, and when he met them, they had the sorrow in their eyes. Some were captains. But they only piloted the river and the harbor. Then he worked in the vegetable markets, trying to help his nephews immigrate from Krk. Then his son died. Then he met Joe, who taught him about cars. Thirty years. Cheated. At first it was why should Joe keep him on the books when John would have to pay taxes and John needed the money? But that meant he wouldn't pay social security. And now it meant no pension. Welfare. But he had known that.

You didn't work you died. He was strong. Margaret would die first; then about checks, money, who would care. Just the funeral. She would die, six months. A year. He'd get a smaller place, one room, a stove, a kitchen. Bathroom. Maybe he'd stay here. Throw out the bed, then paint. Paint everything.

He looked at the kitchen walls, the grimy rivulet-cracks, hawked up a catarrh and spat into the sink behind him. He slapped himself in the face.

Animal, he thought.

"It is time now?" she called.

"Ya, ya," he grumbled. "You sit up and I come. How you feel?" He pulled himself up and moved stiffly toward the bedroom.

"Better," she said. "Look, the sun. Maybe I go out. No, no, go to work. I get up myself." She pushed his hand away. In that instant, another woman, a girl, a phantom young woman with dark clustering hair and ripe heavy breasts pushed his hand away, and a tall young man bowed, clicking his tongue. She kissed his hand. He tapped her cheek, turned, and before he left, heard: "Early, John?" "Ya, ya," he said, and spat into the sink as he opened the front door.

It was a clear morning, with the sun on his back and a cutting breeze coming against him from the Hudson. Up the long street, on either side, the five-story apartment buildings anchored next to each other like old ships; chipped stoops slanting down, façades flaking, windows shaded, curtained, portholes sealing out noise and weather, although now on Sunday it was quiet, with the sun urging itself through the long, dust-and-soot-whirled corridor of the street. A flock of pigeons flapped overhead, soared, wheeled slowly in a frantic white arc and disappeared. He lunged forward, brought the dead leg around in a slow half circle, and before it came to rest, resumed his forward thrust. Margaret's dying was long. He was tired of it. Five years ago he died for her. With her. But she had come back. He couldn't die anymore. It was her death. She had no right to make it his. And to take so long with it. He had more, yet. More in him that she had missed and that now he was being cheated of.

He stopped to catch his breath. Then he remembered he

would be alone at the station, except for Andy, his friend, who had his own job and wouldn't be around much. So if anyone came in needing work on their car he could do it and keep the money and no one except maybe Andy would know.

He remembered the Chevy. All morning and most of the afternoon he lay under the car, putting in a master cylinder. It was an old car. Everytime he jerked at the brake line or tugged with a wrench, the caked dirt and grease crumbled and rained down on his face. By three o'clock he finished, and as he stood up, facing Joe, a small man with a tense, dyspeptic face, he said, ha, that bitch done.

"About time."

"Hey, what you expect," he said, "that piece junk."

Joe removed his glasses, wiped them, as if he were going to preach. "A two-hour job."

"Ho, you t'ink so." He lowered himself onto his wooden milk box. "I like to see you do that in one day."

In the evening, when they closed up, Joe counted out fifteen dollars. "There," he said, "for the Chevy."

"You kidding," he said. "I work all day on that piece junk."

Joe smiled. He was an intelligent man. Had finished high school, started his own business after driving cabs for a while, and John knew the smile. It meant, look. When I make, you make.

"What I supposed to live on, eh?" He was irked and baffled, as when Joe tried once to show him about the credit cards. You fill in this, this, he signs here. But first you check the card against this list. To see if we're supposed to honor it. Right? But it wasn't right, and Joe couldn't read his handwriting, so when they worked together, Joe pumped most of the gas, even though he was the best ignition man on 11th Avenue and had to leave off the work he said brought in all the money to pump five dollars' gas. While John lay under cars, spitting, calling for tools, asking him to raise the jack.

"Don't be a dumb Polack," Joe said, putting his glasses on.

"I no goddamn Polack," he said. "I no li'l Guinea horse cock either. Eh?" Joe smiled and John knew it was finished.

"Look," Joe said. "We don't steal from each other."

"You li'l Guinea horse cock, if I steal from you, oho, you know it. Then you know it!"

"That's right," Joe said, working now on the bills next to the register. He licked the point of his pencil, settled his glasses on his nose. Like a schoolteacher.

"Sure, what you t'ink," John muttered. He moved slowly out of the office into the adjoining garage. He spat into the grease pit on his right and edged carefully along the safety ridge, the piece of steel jutting up on either side of the pit to prevent the car wheels from going over and in. His tools were piled on the work bench in the back, near the disassembled lathe Joe had been trying for months to put together, ever since he had moved from his old store across the street that now was being torn down along with the two tenements, and when the rubble and brick were cleared away it would be a parking lot. The lathe was important, because with it Joe could rebuild starters and generators, which brought in the best money, since he took in the old ones and rebuilt them, and sold them again, and kept doubling his money. But he hadn't the time to work on it yet, and it lay there in pieces, the backboards of dials that John couldn't read, the rubber belts, the steel blade that bit into armatures and threw up a spray of copper bits like sparks that had pitted Joe's glasses for years. Working at the lathe, he looked like a scientist, John thought. And there were his own tools, piled in the middle of the lathe parts, as if he too hadn't yet had time to get his things in order. But the lathe irked him. It was Joe's special power over him, his knowledge. "Sure, what you t'ink," he yelled out. "I dumb Polack?" Feeling it was unfair of Joe, for he himself had suffered longer, harder—for what.

The breeze stopped suddenly. It would be warm, he thought, until three or four when the chill damp from the river set in again. It would be like that until May. As he started forward, two boys emerged from a nearby building. The Kelly brothers. The taller one swatted his brother on the head, and the boy whined briefly, before running ahead, shouting back. "Faggot!" They both wore tight suits. Black hair, swept back from their long faces, was tamped wetly down on their skulls but flapped jauntily as they walked, half ran. Passing John, the younger boy said hello, and as his brother closed behind, started running. The brother nodded shyly; once past, he broke into pursuit. John remembered the long walk through the fields, over the stones and rubble, the constant salt spray in the air, and the dong-dong-dong-dong of the bells from the other side of the island. He would run. Stop. Run. Stopping each time the bells struck, and then running until they struck again.

The Kelly boys. They always went early to church. By nine o'clock the other children would be out, the girls in the Easter dresses, white like birds, and the boys like little horses, hair wet, moving in close groups, voices high. On his Sundays off, he watched them from the kitchen window. He was too old for church, but he enjoyed watching them. If Margaret slept late, he would stay at the window, until he had counted all the heads, and the feeling of church and the remembered pungent

water in bowls and his wet forehead grew vague. Now, exert-
ing himself, he seemed to drag a weight. He felt that someone
watched him too as he watched the children, someone shaking
her head at an old man going to work on Sunday. He scanned
the rows of windows, the façades, the broken stone moldings,
the fire escapes clinging precariously to the vertical walls, and
finally the playground, wedged like pasture between two
buildings.

   If it was bad for him, he reflected, worse for Margaret.
Somehow, maybe, she knew how he felt. A man got tired.

   "Oho," he said. "I work like bull. What you t'ink?" He sat
on his milk box next to the Coke machine. His friend Andy
faced him, straddling his shadow. Across the street, on the
right, was a lone building with a restaurant on the ground floor
that was now shut up. To the left, on the other end of the
block, was another isolated building, a low, one-story place
that housed Patty's Bar and Grill. Between the buildings were
piles of brick and snapped timbers and two walls with the
zigzag stencil marks of missing staircases. Another week or so
and the entire area would be clear, except for the restaurant and
Patty's. Andy worked the Esso station around the corner, but
on days like this he was as much with John or across the street,
scavenging, as he was at his station. He was a quick, nervous
talker with muscular jaws, and he was always grinning. He
waved his arms about, and when he stopped talking, ended
with a little shrug, as if what he said was open to doubt,
though his smile, his fine teeth, and the small shrewd eyes
behind thick glasses and his habit of looking away let you know
he didn't care. Or if he did, he would rather not. He lifted his
beer can to the sun, then bent over in a crouch, as if the beer

when he drank it would dribble down his chin. But he didn't drink. He crouched over and extended the can. He freed one finger and pointed it at John. "You know what I work for?" he said. "Here I am, almost fifty."

John spat. "Ya. You getting old, Andy."

"C'mon. What do you work for? You gotta. Right?" He turned away and drank and faced John again. "I usta like it, workin'. Now I just plain gotta. There's nothin' else to do!" He laughed. "Yeah."

"You getting old, Andy."

"Hey!" Andy protested. "Remember last year when my boss Mike and your Joe was thinkin' about goin' partners? Before Joe got this station? Joe pulls me aside one day by his store. He had this worried look, see, you know, like 'They're gonna pull down my store and all these houses and I'll be on the street any day now, Andy, and what the hell am I gonna do?' So I look at him, and all I wanna say is, 'Jesus. You can live with me till you get straightened out.' He says, 'Hey, Andy. C'mere, I got something.' So he takes me in the back o' the store, by the oil heater, where the cops usta hang out in the winter. And he takes out this booze. 'Here,' he says, 'this'll bring your pecker up. Bourbon.' So we have a shot apiece. 'Listen,' he says, 'I seen Mike's son the other day, workin' the station. He's out of the army, ain't he?' 'Yeah,' I said, 'the little whoremaster. And just in time. Look at that Gulf of Tonkin stuff. We're gonna be at war with those little people. I wouldn't be surprised if it was one of them shot the president last year. Never mind that Oswald crap.' 'Yeah,' he says. 'But listen, what's he do, Mike's son, is he a mechanic or what?' 'Ah, he's just a goddamn grease monkey,' I says. 'Chases snatch.' 'Oh,' he says. 'Have another. Yeah,' he says, 'I noticed him the other day. Listen, Mike's got

all them trucks from up the street, don't he? The theater trucks
that move the scenery and things to the theaters. They got a
good union,' he says. 'Oh, yeah,' I said. 'They got a lot o'
trucks.' 'They have a charge account with Mike?' he asks me.
'Yeah,' I said. 'He's got somethin' goin' with the drivers. You
know, he adds a couple gallons or so every time they fill up. He
adds it to the ticket and they sign it and at the end of the
month he splits with the drivers.' 'Oh,' he says. 'Yeah,' I said,
'he's a real petty thief.' 'Have another,' he says. 'Yeah, I can
feel it comin' up,' I said. He laughs. 'I notice Jimmy the
bookie hangs around a lot,' he says. 'I always see his car at the
station.' 'Ha, ha!' I laugh."

"Ya, ya," John said. "You a real laugher, Andy." Lifting his
eyes rimmed with particles of dirt, he faded, and chewed his
cigar. An old Buick pulled up to the gas pump, and as John got
achingly to his feet, he heard, "Fill it up with three dollars'
worth!" It was Richie Horn, the oldest of the Horn brothers,
who were usually in jail on drunk and disorderly charges, or for
stealing hubcaps off Cadillacs. Richie had been in for nonsup-
port, and as he jumped out of the old car, it started to roll. He
jumped in again—as if it were a habitual motion, jumping
out, then in—jammed on the parking brake, and shut off the
car that seemed to die on the spot. His long black hair was half
in his eyes, and he had a fresh scar on his nose. It was still
Saturday night. John looked at Richie's dazed, half-drunken
grin and the rumpled shirt, then at the girl sitting erect in the
car, pale, washed-out and about eighteen, but staring straight
ahead, sitting in a limousine.

John liked Richie. But as he reached the pump and rang off
the old sale, and as Richie peered into his face, he remembered
he couldn't trust him. Joe had told him, watch out for Richie

Horn, don't leave him near the register alone. Well, Andy was there. And anyway Richie was staying put, breathing in his face. "Hey, John. What's wrong with my car when it dies going up a hill?" John laughed. "What's wrong is you got piece junk," he said. He put the nozzle into Richie's gas tank and squeezed the handle, smelling the sweet-pungent odor of the gas. "C'mon," Richie said. "Free advice." "Ha! You put pedals on it, maybe then you go uphill. Eh?" Richie grinned. "Hey, Lucy!" He called to his girl, who was preening in the rearview mirror. She turned vacantly, tired, her long face, her eyes, her gesture as she rubbed her cheek, all saying what now, Richie? When John looked at her, he felt a twinge of recognition. It was the Brady girl from the house next to his. Only last year she went to church with the others. She brooded a lot, even then, dragging her feet. "What, Richie?" "Meet John," he said. "Sure, I know her," John cut in. "Yeah?" she said, interested now, and sticking her head out the window, the gas fumes rippling past on the air. "Yeah?" "Ya," John said. "I know your father. Oh, long time. Before you born." It was true. He remembered her father worked Pier 83. He worked the docks. But John couldn't remember his first name. He remembered the funeral, and Mrs. Brady leading the children in black. "How's your mama?" he asked. "Oh, she's fine, just fine," the girl said. Ya, he thought. Living on widow's pension. "Hey, don't you live on Forty-fifth?" she asked. "Fifteen years," he answered. "Sure," the girl said. "You got a sick wife, right?" "Ya," John said. "Sure, I know you," she said. He removed the gas hose and hung it up on the pump. "Ya," he said. "Fifteen years I live on Forty-fifth." Richie counted out three dollars in change. He had a handful of quarters, and John wondered where in the neighborhood he had found a vending machine to break open. Richie dumped the change into his hands and said goodbye, but when he got back into the car, the engine turned over slowly, reluctantly, and Richie talked to it, babied it, until finally it kicked over and started up with spasmodic chokes and rattles, and he sped out of the driveway, squealing in a sharp turn, and roared down the street.

"Pigs," Andy said. John sat down on his milk box. "Hey, what you t'ink?" he said. "He work like dog, Richie, his wife got five, six kids. You t'ink he knows how many his? Ha! Two them got blond hair. Eh? How they get blond hair? No good. Lousy woman."

"Broads," Andy said. He threw his beer can into the trash barrel behind the Coke machine.

"Ya. So what Joe tell you, eh?"

"Yeah," Andy said. "I had a girl like that. Usta sleep around a lot."

"Ha! You get plenty, Andy."

"Are you kiddin'? I don' even dream about it anymore."

With his knuckles John rapped on his bad leg. "What you do with this, eh? You still young man."

"Nah. I don't feel it anymore."

"So what Joe tell you?" He spat, and threw his cigar into the street.

"He says, 'I see Jimmy the bookie hangs around a lot.'" Andy leaned against the Coke machine and talked without looking at John. "So I laugh, you know. I says, 'Sure, he pays Mike for parkin' his car. You know, and a little extra somethin' for usin' the phone. He gets phone calls, you know?' 'Jesus,' Joe says. And his face looks like the booze is gettin' to him. 'Yeah, I says, he's a real petty thief.'"

"Two Guinea horse cocks," John said. "Them two. All day they got hands in your pockets, eh? Biggest crooks on 11th Avenue."

"Woulda been a real syndicate!" Andy laughed.

"Ya," John said. "And I work like bull. I know that Guinea thirty years. You know that? One leg, too, I do more than him wit' five. What you t'ink. My son die ten years old. 'Pendix go ploof! I work like hell. And Mar'gret, t'ree op'rations! you know how much that cost? Oho." He spat.

Andy excused himself and went around the corner to his station and the cooler in which he kept his beer. He returned with a six pack, removed a can, and as he opened it caught the spray on his shoulder. He lifted the beer to the sun. "Fuck the boss. All of them." He drank.

"Ya. You drink. Someday Mike catch you and ploof! Why you never get married, Andy? Eh, you getting old too. Too late now, eh? You like me, Andy. Old bull."

They stared across the street.

By late morning the breeze from the Hudson was warm, bringing with it the vague odors of sewage and damp wood. Andy had returned to his station, since after eleven o'clock his corner was usually busy; people visited the big ocean liners at dock along 12th Avenue, and usually passed Mike's Esso station in their cars. But John's street was one way going east, so nothing much happened until late afternoon. Joe would stop by around three o'clock. Just to check things out and see if John had enough change in the register. It was a perfunctory visit and John knew it, but at times Joe seemed to be checking on him and lately it had become annoying. As if Joe thought about nothing but the business, now that his son was in the army. As if he worried always about John doing something after thirty years. The garage was wide open, the pit was available, the tools all there. But then Joe would often have a kind of smirk on his face, and John could see him thinking, well, so far, so good. Ah, he wouldn't try anything.

No? John thought. It was the same with Margaret. Since she'd been sick, she seemed to have died toward him. He came and went, but she closed off to him, closed off in her dying, and they couldn't talk anymore because so many things seemed painful. But she brought them up! Talking about their son all the time, and when he tried to speak, she shut off, as if something had been his fault, and now it was too late, only she, by herself, could set things right. He was out of it. Like Joe, whose son kept calling from the army base down South, kept calling his mother who made excuses to Joe for the big phone bill and Joe knowing his son was being pampered and that his wife drank too much. And he was unable to stop either his wife or his son from shutting him out. But John had no son! He himself was the one dying, laboring back and forth from house to garage. Lunging down the corridors between the old ships, the rusted façades. As if he started walking all the way to Krk, and then had to turn back, because the corridors doubled back on themselves, always back to the house and Margaret, who might be in bed or fussing in the kitchen. And when he couldn't work? When the day came he couldn't get out of bed or the pains never stopped and he would sit on the stoop day after day, watching the kids? There was more yet. He shook his head violently, shaking off his thoughts clinging to him like water. No, he thought. Not yet. He would talk to the social security office, and then force Joe to put him on the books, force him to take the taxes out. Forty years in this country, he deserved a pension. Was it too late? How long did you have to work on the books, before you were . . . legible. Eligible.

He got up from the milk box and went into the garage. He cleared a space in front of the lathe, and laid out his tools. One by one he cleaned them with a rag dipped in gasoline. What, he thought, if he put the lathe together? Right now, when he had nothing to do, and Joe would come and find it all assembled? He poked around in the belts. He found what looked like a series of pipes jointed together and that had small wheels attached with handles on them. Why didn't Joe put it together on his Sundays off? Then there was the board with all the dials on it, and behind the dials all kinds of wires. He cleaned his tools and laid them neatly in his long-handled box. Hell with it.

Bam! There was a tremendous noise behind him, someone shouted, and then what he recognized as a car engine spluttered and died. "Hey, John! Can you fix me up, hey, John?" It was Richie Horn, his pockets jingling like Christmas.

"Oho," he said. "That piece junk dead."

"You know the hill on Fifty-seventh?" Richie said. He swayed from side to side, his hair slipping down toward his eyes that strained as if to keep John in focus. "I was goin' up Fifty-seventh, up the hill. Powie! She started rattlin' and shakin' and she conked out." He waved his hand. "But I let it roll back an' I turned it around and she started again goin' downhill. Like I had a big push, you know, and I went like hell right through a red light, but she started. Jesus." He tottered back to the car and kicked the front tire. Then he put a finger to his lips and turned around, facing John. "C'mon, I got money, fix me up, John." He jingled his pockets.

Lucy sat in the car, looking more fatigued, her hair wisping down along her cheeks. She stared straight ahead, watching the road. John went over to the car, and Lucy smiled faintly at him, the sockets of her eyes grown darker. "Here we are again," she said. "Like bills ya gotta pay." "Ya," he replied. "Ha! I fix this piece junk."

It was an old Buick. The hood opened from the side and had to be propped with a long, arrow-shaped metal bar. But the bar had been snapped off near its base, and he let the hood down again and went back for a piece of broomstick that he returned with and placed between the top of the engine and the hood, which rocked like a metal sail. "Turn it over," he said to Richie, who jumped into the car and tried to start it. It groaned a few times, then whined and actually started, but it chugged and shook and died again. John hit the carburetor with his screwdriver. "Turn it over," he said. Richie tried again. It died. Then John reversed the wires on two of the spark plugs. "Turn it over." The car started, this time banging and coughing and backfiring. "Shut it off." He returned the wires. "Okay, you start it now." Again, it started. It kept running. Richie raced the engine, let it subside. It was still running. "Carb'retor," John said. "You got dirt in your lines. You got little jets in carb'retor, and dirt get in them so no gas get through. I fix it now, it's okay." But the car started to buck and rock. It died again. "Goddamn you piece junk!"

The carburetor had to come off. "You got time, Richie?" he said. "What time is it?" Richie asked. Then he looked at the clock hanging in the office window. "Nah," he said. "I'm in no hurry. C'mon, we'll have a couple beers across the street, the gin mill's open." Lucy got out of the car. She smoothed her skirt, and while she tucked in her blouse, grimaced. "What a mess!" "C'mon, ya look fine," Richie said. John told them it

would take an hour or so. "Hey, what's it gonna cost me?"
Richie said, suddenly shrewd. "Don' worry," John said.
"What you got you pay me." And for an instant his body shook
with a kind of excitement. "You pay what you got." Richie
raised his hands. It was a stickup. "I gotta keep my wallet. Just
leave me the wallet, John." Even Lucy laughed.

He had just disconnected the gas lines, when the long moaning boat whistle sounded and echoed up from the river. Must
be boat pulling out, he thought. Sunday departures were infre-
quent. But a long dock strike had just ended and the sailing
dates of the big ships were days behind. A long, rolling sound,
filling the streets like fog. He grunted, pulled loose the last bit
of linkage leading to the gas pedal, and then loosened the bolts
that attached the carburetor to the still hot manifold. It was
free. He pulled it off and limped over to the gas pumps, where
he turned the carburetor in his hands, then held it up to the
sun, as if the light would pierce it, x-raying the metal skeleton
and showing the tiny shadow of a thrombus. But he saw nothing. He went back into the garage and laid it on the workbench. He started to dismantle it, when a car pulled in for gas,
and the boat whistle cut loose again, this time accompanied by
the high, piercing shrieks of the tugs that must have been
pushing the liner from its berth. The car waited by the pumps.
John turned. He muttered. People were returning early from
the boats. And as he pumped gas into the car, another one
pulled in. He was slow getting to the office and back, making
change, since he never carried the money on him for fear of
losing it or forgetting to ring up a sale. It was slow. Tedious,
because the cars kept coming. He'd get back to the workbench,
loosen another screw, and a car would pull in. He knew it
would last only an hour or so, but each interruption meant he'd

have to start over again on the carburetor, and he'd have to remember where he had left off. But finally he had the carburetor in pieces before him. He pushed back the scattered lathe parts, and peered into the narrow tubes like severed veins in the carburetor's throat. He picked up the air hose and shot air through the tubes. Then he cleaned the outside of each piece with a rag.

"How long, John?" Richie Horn ambled into the garage. He seemed more dazed than ever, and as he approached John, he reached down into his pockets, feeling in a deep hole. He was petulant, his eyes narrow, contracting into red slits. "C'mon, I gotta get uptown." "Ha!" John held up the carburetor. "What you t'ink, I got fifty hands? You t'ink I run back and forth, pumping gas, and I fix this piece junk in five minutes?" Richie swayed. He shot out his hand as if he were stopping traffic. "S'all right. I'll pump the gas. Fair's fair." John limped forward. He came out and looked at the clock. "Ya," he said. "You watch the front."

He was slow getting the pieces together, because the screws were small and his fingers thick. But he managed it. A few cars came in, and Richie pumped gas cavalierly, stretching one arm out behind him, dueling the car, and then wiping windshields with a dirty rag and eliciting scowls and headshakes from the drivers. "Hey, John, how do I work this thing, ah?" He was at the register, pulling down on the handle and banging at the keys. John was leaning over the Buick. He straightened up, and knew the pains were starting again. They began with his leg and inched up his back. "Minute," he said. He went to the register and gave Richie the key that had to be inserted and turned in the register's side. "See?" he said. "You use this key and I finish you up." He limped away and Richie called back.

"Am I gettin' paid for this?" "You pay t'rough your nose you pain in my ass," John yelled back over his shoulder.

Finally, it was done. The engine groaned, but it turned over and started abruptly, the exhaust pipe coughing out what looked like water and oily fluids. "That bitch done," John said, turning to Richie. Lucy had slumped down in the front seat, wagging her head, passing out. Richie returned the key. "How much, you old crook?" John figured it out. For this job Joe would get twelve, fifteen dollars, and maybe three dollars more for a part he never replaced but said he did, showing the owner a piece from another carburetor. But Richie was his friend, and it was Sunday, and Richie pumped gas for him. "You give me ten dollars," he said. Richie reached down into his pockets and scraped around. "Here," he said, and handed John some wrinkled dollar bills. Then he counted out the rest in quarters. He dropped an extra four quarters into John's hand. "Buy a cigar," he said. "C'mon, we gotta go." He tugged gently at Lucy's hair. She groaned and tried to open her eyes, and then slumped down again. "See ya, John," Richie said. He backed the car up, spun the wheel, and sped forward out of the driveway, his tires squealing.

The pains had started. He sat down on the milk box, and leaned against the Coke machine that hummed into his back. He had the ten dollars. And it was almost three o'clock. For the first time, he became aware he had been fighting the clock. And Joe's visit. It starts with a little change, he thought. Quarters. And Joe looking at him, saying how was business? And he would have to think, for me good. For me is good. But how long, how much? He remembered Joe lost his shirt years back when he had a partner in another station. Something about books and percentage and who paid for what. Ha, he thought, it was Joe's story. For his pride. No, it was right. Because Andy told him the same thing, before Joe had mentioned it, and Andy had found out from Mike who was second cousins to Joe's partner.

Thirty years! Margaret had been an okay Catholic before she got sick. What if he said to her, here is ten dollars I steal from Joe. Long time ago she would have cried maybe. Now. She would say nothing. Or she would ask him, you hungry, John? Eat.

The day had warmed up and in an hour or so would begin to cool and the breeze from the river would be pungent and chilling. He sat on the milk box, feeling cranky and stuporous, thinking, long day. Later, Andy stopped by. Going to close up, he said. Things were dead. Besides, Mike his boss was out on his boat somewhere fishing, and he didn't come around like Joe. He walked back across the street. For a nightcap, he called back, his face tan, broad. John remembered he hadn't eaten, so he asked Andy to bring back a sandwich. He listened to the traffic-light control boxes clicking, the lights turning red, then green then yellow then red, up and down 11th Avenue. By morning the street would be clogged with traffic, the trucks shooting up diesel exhaust fumes and the roiling black smoke. And he and Joe would start the day. Together, with their morning coffee, Joe peering through the coffee's steam, as if thinking, organizing, though the station would be empty.

An old blue sedan with its fenders rusting along the body seams pulled in. It was Joe, and he was dressed in his Sunday clothes, meticulous, his pants creased to blades, his shirt immaculate, closely fitted to chest and back. His head was bald and tanned like Andy's face, his short arms gnarled with muscle. He was a small man, but walked with a kind of swagger,

stopping now and then to hitch up his pants. It was a needless
gesture, a nervous mannerism. But it seemed to give him time
to think. "Hi, John." His voice was tired. "Not much doing. I
just saw Andy. How do you feel?" "No good, Joe," he replied.
"No good." Joe looked across the street, then up, sighting the
sun. He shaded his eyes, brushed his hand over his head, and
then held his hand up and studied his fingernails, which today
were clean. "Slow," he said. "C'mon, we'll close up." He
waved John toward the office, and went in and opened the
register, using a key on his chain of keys. "You're out of
singles," he said. "No," John said, pulling himself up. "Can't
be. Had goddamn hundred cars from boats." He went to the
register and looked at the drawer divided into slots. The large
bills were held down by a hinged weight, but the next compartment was empty, and Joe lifted the weight and let it drop
with a hollow *pock*. "You're out," he said. John felt the dollar
bills in his pocket, and the change. A sudden anger flushed
through him, clearing away all pain and stiffness. "Oh, ya,
ya," he said. "I get plenty big bills." He pulled out the dollars
and the change, even the four extra quarters. "I almost forgot,"
he said. "I fix Richie Horn's piece junk. Eleven dollars." He
dumped the change in the drawer, and laid the dollars carefully
under the weight. "For what?" Joe asked, taking off his
glasses, and while he polished them, looking up at John.
"Carb'retor. I took whole damn t'ing 'part. Piece garbage."
"Use any parts?" Joe asked, replacing his glasses. "No," John
said. "Just clean up tubes, you know? He got 'em stuffed like
garbage can." "Oh," Joe said. "C'mon, we'll close up. You get
yourself home." It was like all the other nights they closed up,
John thought. Joe would seem concerned, maybe he had called
his wife and hung up, mad because his son had called again

from the army base and reversed the charges and his wife was a little drunk and crying about her son, and he would pace around the garage, or he would shove the lathe parts back against the wall ("Fuckin' mess") and then he would clean out the register, forgetting the cigarettes that burned out and charred the glass covering the counter. Sometimes he would give John an extra five dollars because it was a hard day, and John would feel the advantage of being paid for each job separately, instead of getting the same wage every week, like Andy. But those days were seldom. The hard days were rare.

"You're four dollars short," Joe said. John was in the back, putting his tools away. "Jesus Chris'!" he shouted. He was filled with shame. He dropped his tools noisily. "Everybody steal!" he said. "Goddamn everybody steal." "Musta been the big bills," Joe said wearily. "If you just go slow, John, you won't get confused." He brushed his cigarette, which was already dead, off the counter. "Well," he said. "C'mon. We'll worry about it tomorrow."

Walking back, he was tired. It wasn't the work, he thought. It was being old. Just being old made him tired. He lunged forward and dragged his foot around. The stoops and façades of the buildings, catching the late sun now, looked dusty and pitted. The familiar breeze blew against his back, with that salty chill, the kind he used to feel on the island, just around sunset. But there were hours of daylight left here, and he was angry with himself that he made such comparisons. Long time ago, he thought. Long time. Thinking of Richie and Lucy, he began to ache. It spread up his back, down, in a kind of rhythm. Now, he would know better. He stopped to catch his breath, and as he put his hand to his chest felt something like crumpled paper in his breast pocket. He hit it once, twice. The money? He had forgotten to ring up one? two sales?—everyone buying just enough to get them home. Where it would be cheaper. He was so busy fixing the carburetor before Richie came back, busy pumping gas, that he had stopped going to the register for every sale, and had put the bills in the pocket where he kept his cigars. But why hadn't he remembered?

He shook his head. Reaching his house, he made his way up the stoop and then up the narrow staircase to his flat. He pushed the door open. Margaret was sitting at the kitchen table. She wore the flowery housedress he had bought her two years back, after her last operation. It was for coming home, he had said. It was to wear at home, instead of the shroudlike hospital gowns. She smiled at him, her hair brushed back, her face broad and tired, showing the kind of strained cheerfulness she had used years ago, he remembered, when their son had died. Her breasts were old, hollow udders, but she lifted up her arms and extended her chin for a kiss. "So early, John? You shouldn't work on Sunday. Look." She pointed to the stove, and after he leaned over to kiss her, he looked behind him. She had made dinner. It was only a stew, but she hadn't made it in months. The lid danced lightly on the pot, and the steam came out sweet, quiet.

"So," she said. "Was it busy?"

"Ya, ya," he replied, holding the table and lowering himself into the chair. He reached into his breast pocket and drew out the four dollars. "I got big tip," he said. "I fix Richie Horn's piece junk. He give me big tip."

She smiled weakly.

SISTERS

1971

Their brother, Eastwick, had promised them a surprise, and Amelia hoped it meant money. She and Elizabeth stood on the elevated Ditmars Boulevard last stop of the BMT in Astoria, from which trains clattered and squealed back to Manhattan, then to Coney Island. Elizabeth, puffy from weeks of confinement, was pleased her phobias weren't acting up, and she'd not once suggested they turn back, looking instead through the streaked windows of the station platform toward the Triboro Bridge behind them, admiring how lights strung on the cables made two beautiful loops over the East River. "Look!"

Amelia thought she meant the flow of traffic on the bridge, and said, "Aren't you glad we don't drive?"

Elizabeth stared at the bridge towers and turned and said yes she was. Amelia was adjusting her coat, tugging at it here and there, glancing at the hemline to see if her dress showed.

Elizabeth shook her by the arm. "Will you please stop that?"

The train pulled in, brushing them back, and Amelia held Elizabeth by the hand while the passengers disembarked. They took a corner seat opposite black graffiti on the engineer's compartment and settled in to wait for the conductor's squawks over the PA, the snapping doors. They were going to 59th Street, to change for the IRT. Elizabeth with her recent weight gain looked like the older sister. Amelia continued to fidget in her birdlike way, as if she was the one recently out of Creedmoor. But it was Elizabeth who would suddenly get dreamy, her speech thick from the three-cornered pill. "I hope he's not going to ask us to move in with him again, like the last time when he bought that awful house." Elizabeth shivered in her lightweight gray coat, the only one that fit her now.

Amelia patted her hand. "He probably got included in a new catalogue and wants to surprise us with how well he's doing."

"It's the only time he ever calls us." Elizabeth drifted, reading opposite her an ad for gin, with the man in it dressed like a Renaissance prince.

"Oh, he's very busy, that's all it is. It's the way he is, busy and forgetful." Amelia wondered if she would ever forgive Eastwick for spending their father's insurance money on the business that had failed and left her and Elizabeth with nothing but her job in Martin's Paints and Elizabeth's disability checks. And now President Nixon was freezing wages and prices, as if it wasn't enough last year to shoot students, to promise to end a war that never ended. She and Elizabeth might have had their own house by now. She might have married Martin Cordes the grocer and had children and lived over the store and rented Elizabeth a room like the one on Crescent Street that she herself had fled to when she tried to leave Elizabeth on her own.

"We brought them, didn't we?"

Amelia reached into her purse and rattled two amber vials of capsules and pills.

Elizabeth sighed. "I don't think I'll need them. I'm doing pretty well, aren't I?"

"Yes, dear," Amelia said. She began to fidget, plucking at her coat, pinching the material here and there, pulling off lint like nits. It was a complex choreography and would terminate only when Elizabeth said, as she did, that Amelia was making her nervous. A middle-aged man entered the train at 30th Avenue, his eyes bloodshot and wattles forming at his throat. Amelia smelled the whiskey and wondered why it was the fumes always carried such distances. And why did they always sit opposite her? The man, not much younger than herself, lowered his chin into his chest and fell asleep.

"Amelia, please stop that!"

Amelia took Elizabeth by the sleeve, and they slid down the long seat toward the door. The car was still nearly empty. She tried to fold her hands in her lap, as Elizabeth, enjoying the return of her ability to read that somehow always revived whenever she was in hospital, read aloud the advertisements for employment agencies and ointments and mouthwash. Amelia knew it would be only a matter of weeks before Elizabeth complained about the print swimming in the *National Geographic*. She herself would have to read the TV program aloud each night, and then Elizabeth would insert the audio plug in her ear, the color picture flickering for hours in silence like a muted life-support system, while Amelia read and drank tea and smoked cigarettes and later took out the dog.

The man shifted, muttered, suddenly popped open his eyes, hiccoughed, and went back to sleep. Amelia wondered if he would sleep past his stop. Here she was regretting Martin Cordes who might have turned out like this. With Elizabeth home now, there'd be new sweaters and blouses and skirts to buy, since Elizabeth couldn't fit into even the old large-sized ones hanging in the back of the closet, where Amelia put them, knowing Elizabeth's cycles would never change and that Elizabeth would never buy anything in the thrift store. "I know what kind of life they had. I can feel it when I put on their clothes. I hate it." Here Amelia herself was, a pinky knuckle swelling with arthritis, ligaments in her hand strained from lifting paint cans in the store, friends like little Adelaide shying away because how often can a person come with you into pinesol-urine halls and sit on a long wooden bench next to a woman who'd cut her hair in shreds and was weeping like a drunk? A goddamn nervous wreck. She began tapping her foot. Martin wasn't so great.

Elizabeth stopped reading aloud. "Did you take Sandy out? That's all I thought about, taking him for a walk. I felt so good. But the way he pulls on the leash. I don't know if I'm up to it." She turned to a new ad. "Do you think Eastwick will be happy to see me? I'm glad you didn't tell him."

So was Amelia. Besides, he had probably been out of town, at his flea markets, selling his little pewter people. "Yes, dear," she said. "Don't worry about Sandy. You can't expect to do everything at once." She patted her sister's hand, and Elizabeth nodded and said, yes, she'd be able to do everything soon. Amelia studied the graffiti on the engineer's door and next to it a man's name. What kind of need was it to have one's name read by thousands of strangers? What kind of need was it that flared and cooled in a woman, and she thought of a poem fire and ice by someone. You'd think doctors knew something by now. Maybe if Elizabeth wrote her name in the subway cars, she'd have no need to see it written in clinical reports.

"Look at that!" Elizabeth pointed to a column of black

smoke rising through the elevated trestle. An old frame house
was on fire below, on 31st Street, and a dark, acrid fog brushed
past their windows. Amelia had just enough time to look out,
straining her neck as she peered down, to see the color of the
house, gray, and its upstairs windows breathing flame. They
heard fire engines blatting and roaring beneath the noise of
their train. A pity, she thought. Even though these houses
were next to the El, even though the trains racketed past day
and night, buzzing the windowpanes, forcing a person to ad-
just her heartbeat to the rhythm of arrivals and departures,
still, many of them were nice houses, neat, clean, possibly even
with a small apartment that provided an income. She began to
pick at the lint and dog hairs on her coat. She glanced at
Elizabeth who was pronouncing "hemorrhoids" from an ad.
Two young black men got on at the stop before Queens Plaza.
They scowled at the sleeping drunk and moved to the middle of
the car, where the thin one began talking about ergonomics.

"Do you think I'll be afraid in the tunnel? Did you bring
them?"

Amelia opened her bag again to display the vials.

Elizabeth leaned against her and whispered, "Doesn't he
stink?" Then she straightened up, and pointed to the third
floor of an office building, the lit windows, rows of desks, on
the same level of the train as it curved away from 31st Street
toward Queensboro Plaza and the tunnel into Manhattan. "I
used to work there, Amelia. Remember? God."

It startled Amelia to remember there had been a time when
her sister could hold a job. That tall, dark young woman with
an English jaw from their father's side, and a talent in art from
no one's side, who was quick-tempered, who laughed, who
gossiped with Amelia about her dates with Donny Clendenon,

the muscular young man who wanted to be an engineer, who thought Elizabeth was beautiful. Who disappeared years ago, even before Elizabeth's all-night binges, the hours of nonstop talk, the terrors, the pills. Before she had ripped the caps off her front teeth and thrown them in the trash can—looking like a vampire, her filed incisors pitiably tenuous in the gaping hole of her mouth. Before Amelia tried to move away; the room in the basement, the house owned by a Greek-American couple. A quiet, tree-lined street, within walking distance of Elizabeth, but far enough away. She could hear the father tell his children, "You don't bother the nice lady in the basement." That room with all its exits and entrances. A front door opening onto a small flight of stairs to the street and a broken chain-link gate. A back door leading into the furnace room. A staircase behind her studio couch leading upstairs to a door with no lock that led to the family hallway between the kitchen and their staircase which led to their bedrooms. All those doors and stairs. And then two boys pulling at her purse on the nice tree-lined street and calling her names and ripping the purse away while she cursed and felt her arm almost pulled out of its socket. And the policeman later asking if they were black when they weren't.

Elizabeth was leaning against the window, hands in her lap, and she turned to whisper in Amelia's ear, "What do you think the surprise is?" Amelia had tilted her head back and was gazing at the ads above without reading them, knitting and unknitting her fingers. Elizabeth, so much taller than Amelia, began to drone from a height. "Little Adelaide hasn't come to see us yet. If I was her I wouldn't come to see me either. I'm a tub. Look." She held up her long hand and wriggled her fingers. "They're so puffy with water I can hardly button my coat." Her tone, in someone else, would have been boredom, condescension, the voice of doctors who Amelia had sat so often in front of. "Your daughter is a very . . ." one had said, outside the locked ward in Elmhurst General. She had yelled at him, "You mean my sister!" her little body gathered into a furious knot, exploding. She had held her hands almost comically over her head. "Wait a minute! Wait a minute!"

"Well, I don't know," Amelia said. "You can't tell with him."

"No. You can't." Elizabeth seemed to lose interest and began massaging her fingers, saying, "This little piggy went to market . . ."

Amelia looked at her watch. What did he want? His business was doing well. He'd been in three more gift catalogues under "E. D. Ferris Sculptures." There was his little statue of Shakespeare reading a book. There was the dog carrying a newspaper in her jaws. And the tree with a boy and girl somehow attached to it that Eastwick called "Eden." He had years ago changed his name from Henry and converted two rooms in his apartment into work and storage space. It was there he designed, manufactured, and assembled the pewter figures displayed in gift catalogues. She'd met him once at a flea market on Queens Boulevard, where he had brought his festively decorated pushcart, and wore his funny hat, and blew on the whistle he'd attached to an upright rod. He was singing ditties, tooting the whistle, and grinning so widely she thought he'd been overtaken by illness—short, grown plump, his hair quite thin, his eyelids wrinkled and loose so that they pushed upward in myriad folds, his blue eyes darting side to side, as he chuckled. It was like him to do this, to appear the fool. In his heart. In his heart, an emptiness, and in his eyes.

"I hope he's not going to ask us to move again. Do you have any gum or something? I'm so dry." Elizabeth made unpleasant smacking sounds opening and closing her mouth. "God." Amelia dug out a rectangle of sugarless bubble gum, unwrapped it, and placed it in her sister's extended hand. Elizabeth began chewing, saying, "Umph."

"We can't anyway," Amelia said, placing her purse between them. "We can't afford anything." She tried to emphasize the last word, without suggesting their funds were dangerously low. Or that it was Elizabeth's fault. Or that they couldn't afford Sandy's dogfood, though she'd been reading about old people living on Alpo. She didn't want to imply that she couldn't get credit in the grocery run by that Indian man.

"You got anymore? I need another one." Elizabeth was sucking her cheeks together, and Amelia withdrew another stick of gum and placed it in her sister's hand. *You got a nickel?* Things tumbled together. Just as she again began thinking of Martin Cordes, Amelia remembered brick high-rises separated by lawns and curved driveways, with only the fences and the gratings on windows to suggest an institution. Inside, the flaking green walls, the elevators with double doors and locks; the abandoned reception area on the first floor; odors of canned vegetables and Salisbury steak. People sat on benches along the path that led up to Building #31. They almost looked normal. The black man in dungarees, the middle-aged woman in the green coat (too heavy for September), the boy who looked up at the sky and who but for an odd wobble of the head appeared as capable as herself. Every time she went, the same woman, her age indeterminate, dark-blonde hair stringy, dirty, uncombed, as if she'd pushed through a briar patch, eyes bleared. "You got a nickel? I just need five cents more." Several patients lounged near the empty reception desk, observing her response. She knew what would happen if she gave in. They'd ask for cigarettes. A ride home. A pencil. She knew what giving the first nickel meant. "No dear, I have no money." The woman wandered to the front door, out into the path, looking for visitors. The other patients wandered off as well.

"Do you remember when I worked for the pickle company?" Elizabeth, chewing vigorously, turned away from reading the ad about pickles, where a stork resembling Groucho Marx held up a jar many times the volume of his body. The train had come to a halt at Queensboro Plaza, hissed open its doors, and was waiting for the arrival of the express. "I could have been a supervisor. Do you remember that?" She poked Amelia.

A four-room apartment with the old pull-chain toilet in the building on 28th Avenue. Windowpanes loose from dried-out putty. Their father's bedroom off the kitchen. The fire escape outside the bedroom she shared with Elizabeth since Eastwick was married and living in Bala Cynwyd and the downstairs cat came up the fire escape to their window bawling for the bits Elizabeth gave him. Father smelling of tires and motor oil from his job at Strauss Auto Parts and asleep over the detective novels he read by the score, the odor from his bedroom of something unwashed and sad ever since mother died, her breast cancer sudden, absolute, unexpected in a thin woman so active, her blue eyes and smallness like Amelia's and Eastwick's, and Elizabeth's olive skin and quick temper from father who was dark and handsome, though his father had had blue eyes, his mother, their Nana, still visiting them, though with the wine on her breath father would shout at her and later fall asleep over his book, the scent of Goodyears blending with his mother's port, and the girls holding their noses, giggling, until he awoke and said, "What's going on out there?" Nana already asleep on the couch in the small living room with the Admiral TV and combination Philco radio/phonograph, Mr. Stokowski the baker downstairs singing in his baritone and the planes thundering overhead going to LaGuardia Airport or her friend Bella's Uncle Frank the iceman roared with laughter that poured out of a first-floor window, into the alleyway, and Elizabeth said she didn't know how much she liked Donny. Amelia said it didn't matter and they put their hands over their mouths when Mrs. Webster next door was screaming and pulling the stove out of the wall because she had five children and a photographer husband home from the war with one leg, and his enlargement equipment filled up their bathroom. You didn't have room to sit and pee. Their mother's best friend, Elsie Webster, a big woman who said she'd be their mother now. Bitsy sitting on the couch, rocking forward to her knees, and back, banging her head into the small depression she'd made in the upholstery. Louise who spoke so low no one could hear her. Little Leon with the rock-like head other boys liked to beat on. Baby Eddie. And Sally, the oldest, her big breasts the talk of all the boys who hooted and guffawed.

"I just hated it!" Elizabeth said. "And the smell. God." She emerged briefly into clarity and anger that Amelia hoped would last until they got to Manhattan. At least to 59th Street. The train sat, humming, doors open, a few more people drifting in. The woman wearing a hat like the one Amelia remembered on Nana—a kind of black beret fastened to her thin hair with a long hatpin—sat down away from them, a shopping bag tucked between her legs.

"I'm getting nervous." Elizabeth leaned against her sister. "Look." She extended her trembling hand for examination.

"It's just the waiting," Amelia said, taking the hand and bringing it down into Elizabeth's lap. "You're doing fine. Just think of something pleasant." She tried it herself. "Little Adelaide said she'd like to take a Circle Line cruise around Manhattan. I'll call her."

"Yeah, sure. We can all jump in the river." Elizabeth exhaled with force. "Why not." She leaned forward, as if to put her head between her knees. The woman with the beret tried to move further into the steel armrest she was already pressed into. "Jesus." Elizabeth seemed to address the floor. "I can feel the blood enter my head. My *brain.*"

Amelia was thinking about money. Thirty thousand dollars. Gone. Like that. Eastwick's embarrassment, his upper eyelids wrinkled and pouched, his ear lobes pendulous. A grossness overtaking him. All that money in his ad agency that was going to return their money doubled in less than two years. In the beginning, his contacts from previous jobs, the one with UPS, a soft drink firm, an oil company. His ads appearing in *Good Housekeeping.* Then terrible things like the war and the arithmetic of dead bodies. His drinking worsened. Elizabeth's condition. Their incredulity as the admitting psychiatrist told them conventional therapy wouldn't work. Eastwick's horrified expression. More drinking. His promise to help and his protests he couldn't take this. Not this. The woman doctor leaning over her scarred desk, in her thick European accent telling them how important they were to Elizabeth. How much she loved her brother, the very man who sat trembling and nodding, while Amelia felt excluded even as she knew who would take Elizabeth back and forth, who would hold her hand after the electroshock treatments and tell her she seemed so much clearer (which she did), Eastwick spending his nights in terrible arguments with his wife, weeping, drinking, threatening to drive his car into a crowd of people.

Elizabeth sat up, the blood draining from her face. "God." Amelia noted the small pits in her sister's cheeks. She'd not thought about or noticed them for weeks. She remembered how they'd worked on Elizabeth's body. Vitamins. Tests for hormonal balance because her cycle was so irregular and she bled so much or not at all. No salt or sugar. Elizabeth improving, until one night as if from boredom she sat down and said, "It can't be that, it can't be that. I'm hearing voices. Voices!" And they both were frightened, Amelia now so anxious there were days she too was almost afraid to go out, and she thanked God she had to go to work. But they kept at it, as if somewhere they could find the rotted place where Elizabeth's mind had become unmoored. They surmised that if Elizabeth felt better about her appearance, she could go out more regularly. So they had her skin scraped, to eliminate the pits incurred by acne. For weeks, they watched the raw, red patches healing on her cheeks. And hoped she'd be able to walk down Steinway Street to look in shop windows or take a bus by herself. That was when she ripped the caps off her teeth—so recently paid for by Welfare (she still needed bridgework for two missing teeth). Amelia frightened for the first time because Elizabeth raved and threw the toaster against the wall, like Elsie Webster, while Amelia kept all the pills and structured each day around the probability of an episode; whether Elizabeth had enough cottage cheese on hand for her constant dieting (whether the new medication did not forbid the ingestion of cheese); whether that first analyst years ago who in addition to his treatment had become Elizabeth's lover for two weekends, whether that man should not be found and shot.

"Will you please stop that!" Amelia had been trying to turn

down Elizabeth's collar but Elizabeth pushed her hand away.
Amelia sighed. The train just stood here, and Eastwick would
be polite but irritable. She imagined how he'd take their coats,
swinging them over his arm, chuckling, saying it didn't matter that they were late. When it did.

Hours later, in the bright light of the 59th Street station,
Elizabeth, her coat open, was looking down at her stomach,
touching it tentatively. "I think the chicken made me sick."
Only a handful of people had changed from the IRT. A man
with dark circles around his eyes was rubbing the arm of a large
woman with orange-red hair who laughed loudly. Several teenage boys were shoving each other playfully down the other end
of the platform. Elizabeth licked her lips, then brought her
mouth down into an expression of sadness, like the mask,
Amelia thought, on a high-school drama textbook. (Amelia
was always the intelligent one, Elizabeth the talented one.
"Born with a book under her arm," their mother said, "and
this one drawing pictures of the doctor holding her upside
down.") One for tragedy. One for comedy.

"Ugh." Elizabeth seemed to be tasting something sour.
Amelia reached into her purse for the foil-wrapped antacid
tablets, freed one, and said, "Here," lifting it to her sister's
mouth. Elizabeth closed her eyes and took it. "If you chew it,
it'll get into your system faster," Amelia said, snapping her
purse shut.

"You know I can't stand the taste," Elizabeth said, opening
her eyes and staring at the black "59" on the support post in
front of her. She shivered and closed her coat. "What if I get
sick in the tunnel?"

"You won't. Just don't think about it. Think about something pleasant." Amelia leaned gingerly over the platform,

looking for the train. Elizabeth pulled her back, and Amelia struggled out of her grasp. "Don't do that!" Amelia scolded.

"Well, don't you do that!" Elizabeth put her hands over her face and sobbed. "What's wrong with me?"

Girls, come in! Eastwick had kissed each of them on the cheek and told them to have a seat in the small living room he'd brightened and enlarged with mirrors on white walls. Amelia hated having to see herself everytime she stood in this room. And Elizabeth's furtive studies of her own image did nothing but darken her gloomy mood on seeing how deteriorated she looked, though with the extra weight, and in spite of periodic agitations, she seemed, Amelia thought, languid and removed. More bored than frightened. A bit spoiled. And as she tried to keep the attention off herself, watching Elizabeth smile wanly at the approaching white cat Eastwick had named Miranda, Amelia was startled to hear her brother conversing in low tones with someone in the kitchen.

It had been easy to conclude that Jessica was the surprise. A stiff-necked blonde woman with a round face like Eastwick's who often brought her hand to her mouth in mock dismay like the English actresses Elizabeth watched on Channel 13. Eastwick's broad, pinkish face lit by wine and excitement, his neatly trimmed mustache and designer peach shirt with thin stripes and French cuffs, almost out of fashion, reminding Amelia that this man wore party hats at flea markets. Jessica, a high-school guidance counselor, had met him at a handicrafts fair in Rockland County and thought him immensely amusing (the way she said it, like Joan Greenwood in *Kind Hearts and Coronets*). But she talked with her chin dropped to her chest, staring at Amelia over her glasses, smiling demurely, and sounding, too much for Amelia's taste, like one of the social workers she was always sitting with, while doctors' names were announced over the PA that was chiming *bong bong*. And Elizabeth saying, "You devil, you didn't say," prodding Eastwick and putting on her best goofy smile (it was always that, when she tried to conceal the missing eyetooth, curling her lip over the vacancy), Jessica laughing rigidly, her blue eyes as steady in their gaze as Amelia's.

"Here." Amelia opened her purse again, stepping further back from the edge of the platform. "I've been saving this." From the plastic vial, she dumped a blue three-cornered pill into her hand. Elizabeth scowled. "I thought I had to wait another hour." Amelia assured her it wouldn't matter. She had gotten so excited she'd used up the previous dose, her metabolism was up, it was the right time, biologically speaking.

Elizabeth threw her head back and exhaled violently. "How can I take it without water?"

"Just let the saliva collect in your mouth, then one, two, it's down."

"I can't, my mouth's too dry from that tablet." It was like the afternoons Amelia would call to remind her to take the two pills on top of the refrigerator. One for anxiety. One for depression. She never left more than one dose in the house. And Elizabeth would resist. Why didn't Amelia leave the pills in the house and she'd just use them when she needed them? Amelia reminded her the pills had to be in her system for days before they would work. They had to be taken regularly.

"I'm feeling better," Elizabeth said. "I am. I think I am."

Amelia returned the pill to its vial, and began to pluck lint from her coat, working up her left sleeve, then the right. She ought to call Adelaide, who usually came over for tea, talking with them in her jittery way, smoking, thin, her hair a synthetic black from the hair salon on Broadway she was always trying to get Amelia and Elizabeth into, arguing against grayness, sometimes talking about men as if her Hank might come back from whatever place he'd taken his good looks to. Some-- times she'd talk about their friend Lucille. Amelia remembered Lucille's flaccid arms around her when she went to see her that last time only a year ago, Lucille's abdomen swollen like a pregnant uterus, her husband Joe moving around the apart- ment as quiet as a deaf nurse, doing everything. Reminding Amelia of herself. Was cancer worse than being crazy? But if she'd been the way Lucille was years ago, outgoing, what would she have said when the doctor with his purplish mouth and creased dark face told her Elizabeth's illness was genetic, a form of schizophrenia, she'd seem normal for periods of time, but . . . ? Lucille would have slapped his face. And that day Adelaide told her, after Amelia described how Elizabeth's cycle varied whereas her own was like clockwork, Adelaide said she, Amelia, could have had lots of children and probably would never have had veins showing in her legs.

Really younger! That's what Jessica had said, talking about her ex-husband and why she'd left him after he'd ruined his knees playing tennis with young women. As little-girlish as she seemed, tilting her head, pursing her lips, shrugging her shoulders, there was something more judgmental in her than Eastwick was aware of. Amelia would bet on it. "Oh, I can't," Elizabeth said, as Eastwick opened an expensive bottle of real French Burgundy. "Of course!" he said, and slapped his head. "Stupid!" He rushed into the kitchen for the small bottles of lemon-flavored seltzer. And Amelia reached over to brush back the coarse, gray wisp of hair that tended to fall over Elizabeth's right eyebrow, replying in the plural when Jessica asked her about herself, "Oh, we have this small apartment, and Eliza- beth takes care of it, and the dog . . ." her portrait of their domestic economy skewed to Elizabeth's putative capabilities.

Elizabeth leaned now against the "59" on the steel pillar, her
dyspeptic spasm replaced by a dreamy thoughtfulness, her
body round and pressing outward in the thin coat. "I guess
we'll be famous now, in that catalogue."

"I hope not!"

"Do you think he really likes Jessica?"

"I think he'll make a fat little statue sitting on a sofa with
her legs crossed and call it, 'The Girlfriend.'" It certainly had
been a surprise. Amelia flapping her hand at the cheeses Eastwick put out and telling him, "She can't have that with this
medication." Elizabeth asking just a little? hovering dark and
plump over the tray of Jarlsberg, Boucheron, and an oozy
wedge of something unknown to either of them. "You know
what might happen," Amelia warned, and Elizabeth annoyed
asked for more seltzer then. But with the seltzer Eastwick came
back pushing a table on wheels, just as Jessica was saying how
once she almost died from eating shellfish, detailing her trip to
the hospital in an ambulance, her husband in his tennis shorts,
limping, useless. Eastwick said, "Ta-daaa!" He snatched the
white cloth away that covered the table—Amelia discerning
beneath the cloth, before he had whipped it off, three peaks of
something poking upward, as if the cloth were really a cere-
ment. All happening again but slowly. Jessica gasping appre-
ciatively. Eastwick saying, "I call it, 'The Sisters,'" smiling in
his professional way, draping the cloth over his forearm like a
waiter, while Amelia and Elizabeth stared. The two pewter
figures were holding hands. One had long hair, or a simulation
of it scratched into a snoodlike tab that hung from a head rather
small for a body made wide by a triangular dress. The other girl
was kicking a leg outward and the dress seemed to billow. She
too had a small head, her cartoon smile and pinhole eyes identi-
cal to the other's. The sisters were not pleased. "Which one is

me?" Elizabeth asked. "I suppose I'm the one with the dress."
She allowed herself to touch it, running her finger along the
edge of the triangular garment that looked stiff as a frozen sail
and was a geometrical variation on the shape of her hair. It gave
the impression that the girl would be swept away in the first
wind, were it not for the sister holding her hand. Eastwick
protested that really it wasn't meant to be Amelia and Elizabeth exactly, and he was hoping for a big run next spring. On
closer inspection, it was not clear why the other girl was kicking out her leg—whether she had lost her footing or was shoo-
ing something like a pigeon. It was difficult to imagine either
girl in an actual physical universe. The figure with the nearly
equilateral dress would never have been able to sit down or fit
through a doorway. The other was doomed to pivot on one leg,
like a geometer's compass, her tiny outstretched foot searching
for contact. Amelia thought the girl in the billowing dress
must be Elizabeth, while the more dowdy figure was herself,
faithfully there, stolid, immovable. She said nothing at first,
watching Elizabeth begin to worry her right cheek, searching
out the small pits that had survived the skin scraping and
smiling in a deadpan way that was startlingly similar to the
expression on the pewter faces. "Are you going to put them in
the catalogue?" Elizabeth asked. It was then Jessica said, "I
wish I had a sister." "Do you?" Amelia responded.

"Do you think she liked us?"

"You were fine, just fine. Anyone would have thought so."
Amelia stepped up and brushed the stray hair back off her
sister's forehead and rubbed from a corner of her mouth the bit
of white powder left from the antacid tablet. "Anyone." And
she thought of Martin Cordes. The early days, when she
shopped for just milk and bread in his store, embarrassed that
other times she went to Grand Union across the street for

specials. He had such a nice smile, and his little accent, and she
never had to ask for credit. Elizabeth was still holding a job,
sharing the apartment, their father dead a few years. Eastwick
using their money. Martin not much taller than she, his bushy
eyebrows, an elfin twist in the corner of his mouth when she
said something witty, his tidy hands at the slicing machine as
he gathered a half-pound of ham off the whirling blade, the
first dates in Italian restaurants where he rated the prosciutto
and mozzarella and told her how much he respected her and
about his late wife a Scotch woman whose legs Amelia remembered were terribly bowed. And he wasn't that much older
than Amelia. But she couldn't remember if their few nights of
sex had been exciting. He was so patient about Elizabeth who
was getting worse and worse. He'd nod and make sympathetic
sounds with his lips that she always thought tasted of cold cuts.
"Well . . ." he'd say again and again. "Well . . ." All she
could talk about was Elizabeth. Elizabeth's moods. Elizabeth's
weight. And that time Elizabeth had come at her and she called
the police who took them both to the hospital where she sat on
a bench near some drunk who'd dropped his pants at a local
bar, and Elizabeth was taken up in the elevator with a nurse
and policemen who had handcuffed her. No harm to herself.
Amelia swore never to call the police again. Never.

"Maybe I should take the pill now." Elizabeth tried to
gather saliva in her mouth, working her jaws as if she were
chewing something, but looking, Amelia thought, like a cow.
"I can't, I just can't." Soon she would begin losing weight,
buying slacks and blouses in sizes she already had in her closet.
She couldn't wear the old clothes, and she couldn't give them
away. "Someday I'll wear them. But not now." She'd talk
about going on job interviews, if she could take the bus, if it
didn't make her nervous. The TV flickering in the living room

where she sat with Sandy the cocker spaniel, his long ears sour-smelling, a dried effluvium in the corners of eyes otherwise forever moist. The syringe-like audio plug inserted in her left ear—the hearing in her right ear damaged from a wrong medication. She *was* hearing voices.

They couldn't agree which of them was the pewter sister kicking her foot out. When Amelia said, "Oh, I suppose you're right," Elizabeth snapped, "Don't humor me. Just don't humor me!" She began to pace back and forth, rubbing her arms. "Listen," Amelia said, "it's coming." They heard a clink in the tracks. A soft rumble. They craned over the platform and peered into the tunnel.

that henry wouldnt & time lost I was taken by extraterrestrials little soft heads like starving children their underwater eyes & fuliginous man with darkness in his fingers the smell of burnt hair the daubed electro-jell did i cry out? tell me if i said anything melia you never talked back to daddy & henry & daddy saying dont run around the house like that in my panties dr esposito in out in out dr dorothy saying softness within you feel your finger a moistness donnys hand his thing in my hand his teeth scraping my nipples donny tongued and i wouldnt no the swelling they bent over me the light round & glaring like a dentists lamp they mumbled because they had no lips their mouths like gauze i heard them i was empty i wasn't no one mrs weber pulling the stove from the wall screaming & me & bitsy on the couch rocking back and forth the voice theres nothing here saying he wanted me eastriver dressballoon god wanted me floating between triboro bridge & hellsgate bridge the trains thumping between black hell lace the girders black lace hellsgate dr espositio said the tunnel the lid closing the dirt dumping thumping i did once i did the voice said open yr eyes the pink lining the satin pillow under yr daddyhead you died i ripped out my teeth before my lips rotted away they had no mouths they had

my time they had white cotton fingers they were children spinning a
rope jumping   my name is alicia im from alabama my name is
barbara im from barbados my name is cynthia im from cincinnati
who i wa wa   the trees green & floating astoria park like a country
in a book like a fairytale   dr expositio said its only a story dr expo
said explaining i you sleep inside the bramblebush has sweet smell-
ing little floribunda white stars & thorns   donny you you   the
voice youll wake oh yes but youre there in the box   i pulled my teeth
away and sank in saltiness estuary that is the something pulling
sucking the tide the tidal knot around the ankles tied he said you
can do me then tied & i wanted him to   dr exponential   dr
mommy someday youll be a great artist   you didnt say that & yr
eyes looking away yr eyes underwater   & daddy carrying a bunch
of mommybones kissing them bones   you wont breathe there   the
noise the noise of buses & trains the woman trying to bite her
arm   the smell   im burning im cooking   im lying on a metal
table   I cant swallow that im too dry melia too   your finger down
my throat like wouldnt you? gagging henry & our gray pewter legs
kicking that woman   & sandy home wagging eating my fingers
only not hurting   down my throat ten at a time in there closing my
bowels opening because I couldnt nails & hair still growing   drool
coming out of my mouth   their cotton fingers pressing my uterus my
lungs nothing on the scale   the top of my skull lifted like a lid so i
could breathe   & dr express changing among the girders the train
taking me   teeth gone   one of henrys jokes mmma mmma w/o front
teeth lips pulled over his gums   their gauze mouths taking time my
time that never was   the voice you bad you bad

"It's coming."

Elizabeth braced herself.

ℒOSERS AND GAINERS

1982

I could show you a graph.

Here he is, at the top, living with his mother in Astoria near the BMT El—his brother out of the house (not a bad sort, but you could see how he looked at him, a little afraid, a little disgusted)—smoking joints like everybody else, but finally limiting himself to two beers a day to show his mother he could control everything. And she'd say she didn't know what she'd do without him. And he smiled.

Here he is, starting down, losing his job at the A&P, because some woman said he told her to shut up, when he was really saying that to a co-worker the other side of the vegetables. Something angry in him getting worse. He's not living with his mother. He doesn't see much of his brother, who doesn't like to come to Astoria. He shows me pictures of his father, a sad-looking man in a kind of brownish light, like in a silent film, who's got his eyes. We're living together because he's left the apartment off 30th Avenue. He's moved in with me because I didn't know he was inching down the graph. I didn't know at his new job he was going to punch an old man who was giving him trouble over rotten fruit. My mother is having fits. I know she is thinking of her sister, my Aunt

Lauren, who disappeared sixteen years ago. She is always worried I'm throwing my life away. My sister Jeannine is saying how could I? She's got me my job in the city so I could quit the Egyptian (who runs a woman's clothing store on Steinway Street. I did this temporarily, after I graduated). He sees how I have to dress in a white uniform, after we're living together a couple of months. He keeps telling me I'm beautiful. He's almost crying.

I think how Arlene has big hips, a big pelvis. She could have lots of kids. Carlos goes for that. So I am not surprised. "I could tell yesterday morning, when I was at the sink. I could tell by the smell of my body. It was fuller. Kind of deep. Full. I don't know. He's a good man, but we don't even have the house fixed up yet. What do you think?" I think Carlos looks at me a lot in the kitchen. I think he's wondering what it's like with someone like me. I think his eyes are hungry. "Oh, Arlene, do it," I say. "Keep it."

It must have been the beer I bought his friend Brian. That was the moment if it hadn't happened a lot of other things wouldn't have. Brian—once with a real job, benefits, vacations, can you believe it?—was rubbing his eyes, telling me about his parents, getting deep into his bottomless cellar. I bought him a beer. I had nice clothes. I was making good money. Jeannine had gotten me a job with a plastic surgeon. All I did was sit in my little white outfit, as if I was a nurse—that's all I had to do, he said, sit, and be beautiful—take names, messages, tell people he'd be with them, bring them coffee, magazines . . . careful not to stare at the hard cases, the burn jobs. The no-faces. The arms like twisted tree limbs.

If I hadn't bought Brian that beer, I would've gone home to my apartment and talked with Arlene on the phone. Or read

the ads for a Caribbean cruise. But in he came, his eyebrows
surprised, his mustache dark and curving downward, his white
teeth, his white, white teeth. I felt my blood vessels open like a
harbor.

Smiling with his whole body. Asking if I minded him working for a moving and storage company. "I'm a mover," he says.
I am so dumb, watching him get huge, never thinking of
steroids. The way he comes at me, like a wall wrapping around
me. "I'm a mover, baby. I make it happen." Changing from
week to week, depending on what he takes, but always a little
voice telling you don't pay attention to this because it isn't the
real him punching the wall, his eyes afraid, and you in the
kitchen trembling all over. Arlene on the phone telling you,
"Get out of there. Just do it."

Here he is, almost halfway down, where the line squiggles as
if leveling off, then it starts dropping again. He's punched the
glass in the bathroom door and I've taken him to the Emergency Room. Some nights he turns to me and asks if he can
brush my hair, and in the morning he makes me breakfast, and
he's the only man who knows who I am. But he's hanging out
with Brian. And he starts laughing through his nose, a kind of
sniggering, as if he's mocking me. His smile has gone all into
this kind of thing. He's like a second you buy from the Egyptian, one of those discount dresses, not knowing it's a second,
believing it looks fine, the seams are good, the colors don't run.
Then one day it looks threadbare.

"If you have kids," Arlene says, "you'll have retards and
cripples." She means he is so fucked up by now from drugs.
This is after her implants have gone bad, they have to scrape
her out, and she loses her nipples. She has these little stars

where they used to be. She wants me to see their house. And I
think how if he comes with me, he'll gawk at the lawn, at
Carlos' workshop in the basement, or her aunt's needlework
doilies. And never think why he doesn't have anything.

You face the fact his eyes have been glazed over for a long
time. He's not looking at you. Or at the scar on his left forearm
that's a livid pink and his fingers are in pins and needles from
nerve damage. He's complaining all the time. He's telling you
there are no jobs but you see them everyday in the want ads.
He's telling you a friend is going to teach him the auto-body
business, he'll learn how to spray-paint cars. The next day he
says that stuff will ruin his lungs.

You can't later imagine him walking with his brother down
14th Street a few blocks from his hotel, saying, "Once I find
the right woman, I'll straighten out." They are passing graffiti
on the New York State Armory wall, and on the other side of
the street the Salvation Army building, the motto with "While
women weep as they do now   . . ." and the little stands with
discount can-openers, socks, tablecloths. Next to signs for
Luggage, Linen, Jewelry, salespeople are calling to pedes-
trians. Odors of hot dogs, sausages and onions mix with the
exhaust fumes of buses. Men are tearing up the asphalt, they're
in pits banging away with pneumatic drills, steam pours from
cavities.

They are just walking under the awning for the Cafe
Zaragoza when he laughs in that snickering way to hide his
thoughtfulness. He hates his brother to catch him thinking.

"What about Bethany?" the brother asks.

"Her? She thinks I'm a charity case. A loser." He snorts. "I
don't need that shit." He lights a cigarette without breaking
stride. "I need somebody like Toni." He laughs. He is refer-

ring to his brother's friend, who recently left him for someone
in Munich but now is back, taking singing lessons. "I mean
somebody who doesn't have a job and an attitude, who isn't
always looking down her fucking nose."

They are walking under the scaffolding of the church being
renovated, *Nuestra Señora de Guadalupe,* the coolness inside
where he will be in a box covered with a white cloth in the aisle
between the pews, where the priest will be all in white talking
about the white mansions of God, where his unshaven friends
in fatigues and bulky sweaters will huddle shyly in the rear.

The brother says, "I don't think you know Toni." Toni is
not able to keep a job, always talking about being a singer, an
artist. Toni likes to lean back and laugh, her long arms raised
like a ballerina's.

"Face it," he says. "You don't think I know anything."

He asks you for money for clothes for an interview. You find
him hanging out with Brian. And Arlene and your sister stand
over you like matrons with their arms folded, telling you,
"See?" And he gets bigger. Thicker. Shaping up every day
down near the El. You're not sure you like this, but his
mother's in the hospital, what can you do?

You're with him one day when he visits her, flowers
wrapped in green paper in his hand. He grins. "Hey!" He hugs
his brother. "What d'you think, Ma?" Holds up the flowers in
his fist. And she smiles in her tissue-paper-thin way through
which you sometimes see a patient weariness. He talks about
Arthur Godfrey, Peggy Lee, John Wayne, the one-lungers.
"As long as I don't have to breathe through a tube," she says.
"Or with that plastic mustache." "Isn't that something about
your mountain, Ma?" He means Mount St. Helens that has

blown out its north wall. His mother's name is Helen. He means the boulders tumbling down to Spirit Lake, stripping willows and black cottonwoods. "I mean, it's cosmic, Ma. You're cosmic." Then she leads him and his brother into the dayroom, where she smokes a cigarette and says, "It can't make that much difference. Now."

Here he is, the line going down, then straightening, the line like an arm bending at the elbow. If he were a stock, he'd be −0.04. You've thrown him out because you gave him money to pay a bill that he didn't pay and he's hiding porn videos in his socks drawer and he's punched a hole in the kitchen wall. But he gets a one-room apartment with the money from his mother's estate. He's given away everything connected to her, given to his brother the pictures, the sons' report cards she saved, the baptismal certificates, the father's social security card with the signature like his.

A few months later, after Mount St. Helens has erupted again, you read how on the slopes the muskrats and minks return, the deer mice, the tailed frogs. The newts and ants and spiders and beetles. Anything with broken branches, able to form roots or sprouts. Also comes the thimbleberry, salmonberry, elderberry.

You remember his goddamn smile melting you down to your knees. His thing about your hair, telling you Chinese women cut their hair when they get married so they won't be attractive to other men. You saying you weren't married. You weren't Chinese. You weren't cutting your hair. And he brushed it for you, stroking down with the nylon prongs, asking if you slept with anyone else. Smiling.

You've dated a couple of guys, the usual thing. You start dating him again because he's down to his normal size, where

you can feel the muscles along his ribs, and his back hard, he's
+ 0.50, and he's sorry. His mother. Brian. He blames Brian a
lot. And the messenger work is temporary. A friend who's a
doorman in an apartment house in the city will get him into his
union.

Arlene calls you and says, "You know, he doesn't care. He
really doesn't care." She means Carlos and her nipples, her not
having them. It is her way of telling you you're involved with a
jerk. Of telling you looks aren't everything. Of telling herself
Carlos being a fat man doesn't have a roving eye, that he
doesn't watch me when she goes into the kitchen. I am just not
in the mood. It is like having my mother on me when I didn't
clean my room, or being relieved I finished high school, which
could have been positive except I knew she didn't think I had
any smarts. Maybe that's what he and I have in common. No
one believing in us.

Then he breaks his ankle, riding a rented bike. Loses his
apartment in Sunnyside. Here he is, starting down again, all
his mother's money gone. He's on the street, meeting me down
from Precious Blood Church, where we both used to go, where
he went to school and his mother thought the nuns would
make him into something. I am giving him twenty dollars
before he goes into a rehab program the next day.

There is a young man waiting to see Dr. Bixby. He has a
terrible burn scar down the left side of his face, so that he looks
fine from one side, but from the other . . . I have to look
away. He has a large pin, round, the size of a half dollar—like
the kind people wear during election campaigns—that says,
"Shit for Brains." I watch him, a magazine open on his lap. I
see from his records he is twenty years old. He works for an

auto repair shop and there is an issue of who is responsible for the cap that flew off an overheated radiator. Whether the steam that ran up his face like something from a hose was his own fault. Or something the insurance company had to pay for. You can hardly tell the color of his left eye, the way it is surrounded by crinkly skin. He sits there, turning this way and that, looking at the pictures on the wall, looking at the wall. I see that he is practicing. He is getting used to people staring then looking away. He picks up the magazine and flips through the pages. He asks me what time it is. He sits like a statue, while the other patients—a boy with a raspberry birthmark on his temple, a woman who seems to have nothing wrong with her, though she sits hunched over, angry-looking—they always look around him, through him. And I think it doesn't matter why the radiator cap flew off. It just did. And he was there, in the wrong place.

Arlene says I've forgotten the way it was. That if his mother had lived, he would have been rotten to her. That something was driving him, something mean, something even his brother didn't know about because all the brother saw was the abandoned little boy, though his mother had never done that, never left him, though his father died, a man who went to Iona, and Fordham Law, who was a lawyer everyone liked. That just because he was out of that place in Long Island City where I found him living on the second floor of a house that had no banisters on the landing, where you could fall and fall, it didn't mean he had cleaned up his act. There with the young couple next door always shooting up. Blood in the hall toilet. But better than the shelter when the lights went out and men made love to each other. Groaning. And someone came at him with a screwdriver the next morning. All these things. All these bad things.

Here he is, coming back up, the point of the line about as
high as an upside-down thumbtack. At least twice he tells me
something bad is happening at the hotel. Drugs everywhere,
guys with needles in their arms he finds dead. He swears he is
off everything. He goes to AA. He thinks he can fool around
with other things. What's the harm? I ask him to make sure,
before he moves back in. Make sure. Arlene knows I am scared
to death. My mother isn't talking to me. Jeannine has her
hands full with a husband just learning to walk again, after
being hit by a car. My brother . . . the cop, who worries my
mother constantly because she's thinking about her brother,
my Uncle David, who was killed in Korea, and she doesn't
want to lose her son in this other kind of war. All those bums in
Port Authority. My brother isn't surprised, he says, that I am
taking him back. He means I am weak. And stupid.

All my life I have wanted to be pious like my father. Every
Sunday, I'd feel a lightness in my walk, a glow in my body, as
if being holy and being happy had nothing to do with what I
heard from the pulpit. It was enough to walk beside my father,
to see his half-frown relax into a grin, and I'd ask him about
God. "You're so serious," he'd say. "Why? Why do you think
God is so serious?"

Arlene hugs me. "Come in, come in!" I blow a kiss to Carlos
who looks a little sheepish in the kitchen doorway. He looks
embarrassed all the time. Maybe he is ashamed being so big.
Clumsy. Filling doorways. Sitting down, half his body hanging over his knees. But he makes a lot of money cleaning
carpets. He has two trucks, which he keeps in the driveway.
He has routes in Westchester and Connecticut, besides Long
Island. Sometimes I can see why Arlene likes him, a man she

can lose herself against, like lying down on a king-size bed, the whole big soft field of him. I can see she has taken the house over, the porcelain things beginning to appear on little shelves, the rugs that are too white, the spotless bathroom sinks that look as if water has never touched them yet, the aunt's doilies, the needlework things that say "I know a bank / Where the wild thyme blows" hung up in frames on the wall.

She takes me by the hand to the small room next to their bedroom. "See?" she says, "pink on two sides. And wallpaper on the other two, something active to keep his mind busy. Or hers." Carlos, in the doorway, laughs. "Hey," he says. "His. It's going to be a him." He laughs again. I feel his eyes on me.

So superior. Asking me when his brother disappeared if I knew where he was, and resenting it, having to ask me. He couldn't stand any of us. A tall man who'd once had acne. Blue eyes like a child's the way they always popped open wider and wider. Maybe it was the contact lenses. When he walked, he kind of paddled the air, his palms facing backwards, but in the apartment he sat with his legs crossed, his hands folded on top of his knees, as if he was waiting for me to tell him something. He was giving me his complete attention. The lawyer. Who you could imagine thinking that his brother would wind up killing himself because he had crummy genes like their father. A man dead in his prime in his office near the public library, a block from Steinway Street, a local lawyer with not such a good heart after all. It didn't matter if one of them slumped over his desk and the other blew the side of his head out. It was something the brother felt no guilt about because a thing was inside them like twisted thread. And the move back in with me had been a hoax.

Shit for brains. But all I had was a few years. He'd had all his life, the brother with the education, who ran from him like he would be tainted. Who probably thinks I killed him. Like I was making a right decision for the first time in my life. And if you asked me why I did it, all I could say was he asked me to because I loved him. He showed me how to hold it, how it would jump when I pulled the trigger, how I should aim a little lower because of that, but not so much it would go into his neck. And I was a damn fool because I really believed he had no future. I took him at his word, that he couldn't stand lying anymore, kidding himself. In that one moment, his face smooth and peaceful, he begged me to keep it true—the moment he could feel he was already losing.

Here he is, slipping off the graph.

$\mathscr{T}$HE SUBSTITUTE

1992

Emily knew it wasn't just her distant consciousness of her infant granddaughter's movements within the milky sides of an incubator. It was also the war in Yugoslavia. In Croatia. That, and her little premature granddaughter, had brought back the old awareness: a silky thinness of her nerves admitting shadows of things that were not there, things from the future or from great distances, so that she shuddered and closed her eyes. And Nikola said, "Why must you do this? It isn't right. It isn't normal."

He was angry, she knew, not because he feared what was happening—he had always admired this shivering transparence in her, this religious something. But he saw that she had become too frail. The TV and the papers carried stories about Vukovar, so near her mother Viktorija's birthplace, the river, the bridge on the other side of which one could see Serbia. She couldn't look at the news photo of the old woman in the back of a truck, her belongings tied up in a blanket, the inky dress dusted by crumbled mortar and pulverized limestone.

Nikola said, "Over there, they kill you for a shovelful of dirt!" He folded the newspaper and smacked his lips, lifted his seamed face toward the ceiling, and sighed. "Why you think I left that place, anyway?" He raised his hands and worked them up and down, as if throwing dirt over his shoulders. "Why you care so much? You don't have enough problems?" He meant himself, and she felt bad.

He was doing everything since they'd retired to a refurbished log house. In fact, they had moved around the same time that their daughter Vera and her husband Walter had bought a house off the beaten path, near a place called Furnace Woods, near Walter's school and close to a county park not far from the Hudson River. Nikola and Emily's house was a good fifty miles north, not far from Poughkeepsie and the upper reaches of the river. Their house perched on a hilly site less than half a mile up from the railroad tracks and the foundation silhouette of an old depot and what was once Mr. J. C. Penney's black angus farm. The road that went past their house continued uphill to a few impoverished homes, one inhabited by a black family that left rusted cars on their lawns, and another property containing the shell of a home that had been started and abandoned. But it was the country landscape that Nikola had yearned for. The old, high lilacs lining the road gave off their pungency each spring, and he had set a row of irises in the earth along the sloped driveway. His vegetable garden spread its rows on the only level portion of their land, just before it swept upward and became a steep, rock-encrusted hill. Behind the house, each August, a few trees yielded juiceless, spotted peaches. The road, which terminated at a narrow plateau with tall utility towers and phone lines, was kept clear all winter by the power company.

Nikola did all the driving. The shopping. Now even more of

the cooking, since Emily's sight was gone in one eye. She was barely able to walk, her feet swollen from arthritis, but when she got gloomy, and now, when he could see that she was having her experiences, her visions, he'd say, "You should get some air!"

He did not, she knew, mean that he didn't care about their granddaughter who—she could feel, she could monitor through the sensations of her own body, though she had never been to the hospital, had not yet seen the infant—was now on her back, moving her wrinkled arms, her head to one side, plastic tubes feeding oxygen into her nostrils. But there were times lately that Nikola reminded her of her father, her gloomy father with his princely carriage, florid and angry after two glasses of wine, in the years when her mother, bent over a steaming pot, stirred soups with a wooden spoon, or rolled up polychinka, the sweet pancakes, filling them with fruit. Later, her father had lived in the basement of the house she and Nikola bought, her mother inhabiting the small bedroom upstairs. Vera was only a baby. She herself, only in her thirties, about to enter menopause, like her mother who had stopped menstruating at thirty-three. Nikola would go to his job at the bakery at ten P.M., after eating the dinner she cooked. And then, with everyone else in bed, she'd do acrostics, holding them close to her eyes, words swarming in her head. That richness reduced each morning to monosyllables, as she discussed the day's menu with her mother, who complained she didn't have enough Crisco. Her father, Matthias, brooding downstairs, because he and Nikola had argued about money the night before.

Tonight as usual, Nikola had gone to bed first, after adding water to the bulbs of narcissus Vera had given them, which they kept in the bedroom on the old dresser. After reading the paper in her laborious way, with a magnifying glass, Emily came in and slipped under the blanket, listening to Nikola breathe steadily in his bed near the window, the fluorescent dial of the clock between them, and his bottle of Tums, her thick eyeglasses, a book of poems. Yesterday, Vera had cried and cried. It wasn't right, to be on a machine. Shirley Ann— named after her husband Walter's dead sister—wasn't a machine. She shouldn't have had such a late child, she said. She was not like those women having children in their forties. She wasn't built like Jane Fonda. But Phoebe and David had been such wonderful babies. Who could have known? And Walter running all over the place since his father's death, visiting cousins in New Jersey, Baltimore, Florida. Even a trip to Israel to see his father's last surviving brother, now an immigrant from Moldova, living on the edge of a desert. Walter, after all these years, able at last to say his father's name without twitching his mouth unpleasantly.

Emily began to drift out of herself. She could feel the vacancy of her body she was departing from and, at the same time, herself rising like a handkerchief on the wind. Was she in Dutchess County, or back in Astoria? The bakery on 10th Avenue? Or that busy street near Arthur Avenue, where her father visited the Croatian produce stand, windows hung with great Italian cheeses?

Her nightgown was soaked. She wanted to turn on the light, but her hands were moist and she was afraid of shock. All her life she had feared electricity. Yesterday morning, when she had awakened to an acrid, stinging odor, like burned wiring, she believed it was coming from Nikola's work pants folded on top of the wicker basket in the corner. But the odor was not that of the solvents and petroleums he used when working on his garden tractor. She had sniffed the air, trying to locate in her memory an object, a place, a time. And just when she realized the odor was coming from the narcissi that Vera had given her—suddenly she saw her father, Matthias Baršić, propped on the satin pillow in his coffin. She smelled singed hair. His cheeks were tomato-red, lips sticky as from cherry cough drops. She was dreaming. Awake. And there was a little girl running about in a dress she recognized as her own, a delicate stitching along the hem, the crinkled sleeves so deftly shirred by an aunt. Was that herself, when Aunt Margaret had visited from Philadelphia? She reached for the child. But there was no one there. Only the burned smell of the narcissi.

And now it happened, for the first time in years. On the end table, next to the poems by Edna St. Vincent Millay—a tiny garnet appeared. In spite of its size, it had many facets and gleamed a deep and twinkling red when she switched on the reading light attached to her headboard. Nikola started awake and called her name, without turning around. "Nothing," she said. "Go back to sleep."

She blinked repeatedly, and faced it with her eyes closed, and opened them abruptly as if to surprise the thing, to repel it. But there it was. The last time had been a sapphire, materializing on her kitchen table in their house in Yonkers the night after her mother's death—a terrible time, since Vera had left Walter, and she and the two children were in the living room, coughing, waking each other up. Emily hadn't touched it, but got up from the table, circled it, studied its little blue heart. In a fit of pique, she had left the kitchen to busy herself with laundry, vexed to find that Nikola had brought home a shirt smelling rancid. She stuffed the shirt violently into a paper bag and left it outside the front door, in the evening air. The odor of the shirt disappeared by morning, and the sapphire had vanished when she returned to the kitchen.

But the garnet was still here. She almost cried with frustration. Last week she had begun, again, to see outlines of light around people in the shopping center, while she sat in the car, waiting for Nikola to come out of the Grand Union. "Oh," that woman had said, years ago, "you're seeing the aura. It's not uncommon in someone like you. It's really just the energy body. We all inhabit one." Why was this coming back on her, and things like the garnet? She reached out and touched it. Cold. As if out of the freezer. She lay back and sighed. She was going to die. That little girl, she'd come to take her away. To kiss her cheek. To lead her into the corridor of light. Something that was once herself. There'd be things to arrange, things Nikola couldn't do. Accounts. Insurance policies. Money for Vera and Walter and the children.

Exhausted, but suddenly warm under the covers, she looked once more at the garnet and fell asleep. She dreamt of the little girl, blonde hair hanging down in curls. The girl was reading out of a book, pronouncing words with great care, just as she used to, trying to correct her mother's foreign accent. Where was her mother? She could face only one side of the room. The child seemed to address people behind her, but she couldn't turn to see them. And there was that electrical smell again. Like the time the brakes had seized in Nikola's old Buick, and she was afraid they would burst into flames, all of them consumed. She watched the child and was aware of herself watching the child.

And thinking: *that odor*. Death. Not the stench of a deer hit by Nikola's car and left in the woods. Death was PCBs, death

was burned wiring, death was the brassy taste of old light
sockets, death was Nikola laughing as the child stopped reading and began to whine, suddenly examining her dress, the
bottom of it stained with chocolate, the kind he always gave to
the grandchildren. What was he doing here, so pleased with
her dying, laughing?

"She's worse," Vera told her the next day on the phone.
"What should I do, Mama? They're talking about a brain
bleed."

"What does Walter think?" Emily was trying not to have a
headache.

"Nothing. He doesn't say anything, Mama. When she was
born, he used to say we'll do what's right. Now he doesn't say
anything. You should see the other babies. The way they
shiver. What if she's damaged?"

"Oh, Vera, I'm so sorry." The entire left side of her body
began to ache. She couldn't help but think of Vera's childhood
illness, the pneumonia, how she herself had almost come down
with it but had fought it off, knowing the seven-year-old child
was the one in jeopardy. This power, this flowing out of herself
was only a swirl that swept everything extrinsic back into her
center, into a transparent knot above her womb, into the well
it became as it dissolved. Stroking Vera's moist forehead, listening to the child's labored breathing, she had upbraided
herself. This borderlessness that a nun once tried to convince
her was the seed of religious life, what was it but a need to
control everything. A devouring selfishness.

"Let me talk to her." Nikola had entered the kitchen, a
coldness coming off him from outdoors, his face pink from
wind. He took the phone. "Listen," he said. He told Vera he'd

spoken to a lawyer. There was nothing they could do. State law. Emily knew he'd been at Senior Citizens, talking with John Tagliabue who, in retirement, half-blind, sat at the tables in the old firehouse, giving advice every Wednesday. A nice man who'd helped them undo the reassessment of their house when they first moved in.

"Niko," she said, "she doesn't need to hear that. Give me the phone." He shrugged and she grabbed the phone before he could start talking about what was not meant to be. "Vera," she said, "I want to see her. I'm going to the hospital. Your father will drive me."

Nikola protested.

The next morning, a letter arrived from Krk, the island where Nikola had been born. His cousin Marija described the refugees coming up the coast from Zadar, from inland, too, near Zagreb. They were being housed in the thousand-year-old church off the little village square in Omišalj where children still played under the chestnut tree. Two families had moved into the narrow, stone house where Nikola had lived with his five brothers and two sisters and his father's mother. Emily didn't want to hear any of it. His hard times. She didn't want to hear about Nikola's Uncle John, who had emigrated from the island and lost his leg in a quarry in Pennsylvania and who had helped Nikola come over. They used to visit him in the nursing home in New Jersey, when he was too sick to work in that gas station, after his wife died. It had been difficult enough, not so many years ago, to stop Marija from sending over the young Tomo, whom she had wanted Nikola to sponsor in America. Now all this talk of the refugees filling the rooms at the Adriatic Hotel, where Marija's daughter worked. Even the old Učka, a run-down hotel built by Nikola's uncle in the 1920s, and used now as a dormitory by the waitresses and busboys from the hotel, was filled with people whose belongings were tied up in blankets. The resort in Opatija—playground of bored, sun-hungry Germans—was filled with weeping children, distraught grandmothers. Emily didn't want to hear it.

"My God!" Nikola said.

She told Nikola they could send a check. But she was remembering another war, when she and her parents lived opposite the funeral home in Astoria. Her father sitting at the kitchen table, head in hands, the letter pushed away from him, unsigned, only two words in clumsy capitals in the Cyrillic she had learned to read and that they all knew had been written by Stanko, a Serb brought up in Croatia, a man he'd worked with for years. She knew what it said. "USTASHE BASTARD!"

She closed her eyes. She tried to be blank. She thought of Shirley Ann but realized there was nothing to see except the shifting light, on the other side of which was a blurry whiteness in motion, probably the nurses. It was not surprising that she could be there, that she could be peering from within the incubator. Or that she could experience these cramps. This pressure in her chest. Again, she had dreamt of the girl, this time playing with a wheel, a brightly colored wagon wheel on the floor. Her dress whiter than ever, the girl danced in and out of the spokes, chanting something that rhymed. And Emily had been annoyed. And relieved. She still had time. The garnet, when it appeared that morning, had had a deeper flush. Like a ruby.

"How do we know if they will get the check?" Nikola said.

Late that afternoon, Vera met them outside the hospital. She was a broad-bodied woman, like her mother, with a beaming smile and a voice that often was loud, bursting from her. Emily hated to be in public with her. Vera was always talking about the children and saying things like, "David, well, you know David, how gloomy he gets." Her voice would lower its pitch but deepen its effect, like a bass instrument. Or suddenly crack, grow thin. "I think there's something wrong with him. And Phoebe, she just dances around like a spirit."

Today she looked pale. Shirley Ann's birth had drained her. She'd looked that way when she had separated from Walter. A girlfriend? Vera never said. And what would they have told Nikola, who allowed so little margin for error? One had to do the right thing. And Nikola knew the right thing. "That's it!" he'd say, waving his hand as if brushing away a fly. "That's it!"

Mother and daughter stood in the parking lot, their arms folded. Emily was squinting her good eye, and Vera pressed her lips together. "I don't think this is a good idea, Mama." Nikola added, "Why? Why you do this?"

"I'll go by myself," Emily said, lurching forward. She extended her hand toward the hospital entrance and advanced toward what she dimly perceived as automatic doors opening and closing. "I can find it."

They agreed that Nikola would wait downstairs, in the room with TV and coffee-maker and styrofoam cups, while Vera took Emily to pediatrics intensive care. Emily could smell the hospital better than she could see it, remembering the old woman in the bed next to hers when she'd had the cataract removed— that diabetic woman who'd lost her feet, who moaned all night, the blood-soaked gauze something Emily still dreamed about. She mustn't think about that woman, she thought. She was here to see her granddaughter. All these brisk young people in white calling her "dear," and Vera saying no one was to blame, though she suspected that Emily blamed Walter, a man she never liked, with his endearing smile, like Vera's, but given to backing away, rubbing his eyes at family dinners, bothered, Vera said, by allergies—while Emily thought it was his way of withdrawing from her and Nikola. All that contrariness in Vera culminating in marrying a non-Christian, in marrying him outside the altar rail in the church that Emily and Nikola had long stopped attending.

It was terrible. The first infant Emily saw was lying on its side, its head swollen and egg-shaped, pink veins like a net holding the soft skull intact. The hands moved as if swimming. The next child was on its back, a respirator tube taped to its mouth. Its chest rose and fell. It looked like a little old man, ribs expanding, the stomach hollow, the arms moving puppet-like with each puff of the machine. Nurses moved back and forth, wearing surgical masks, sometimes inserting their hands through the holes in the incubator's sides, where elastic sleeves hugged their wrists as they turned an infant over, reattached a monitoring wire, or just touched for the sake of touching. One infant lay on its stomach, its pelvis flat, legs splayed outward like a frog's. Another had an indentation in its chest, as if someone had left a flatiron on it. Another, not in an incubator, had a hood over its head, the skin of its abdomen nearly transparent, so that Emily saw a reticulation of veins, while the face remained hidden in the hood filled with oxygen.

The mask over her mouth grew hot and moist as she approached the incubator she had visualized that morning, seeing a white cart being pushed past, a whiteness flashing across her vision like the mark of a sponge. When they reached Shirley Ann, Vera turned away, unable to speak. Emily was not surprised by how tiny the child was, the skin wrinkled like latex, the feet twisting as if seeking purchase, wires and tubes taped to her body. What shocked her—aside from the raspberry blotch on the right side of Shirley Ann's face—what caused a thrill in her nerves was the dark approximation of her father's scowl in the infant's physiognomy. Her father's image so instantly flashed upon her, she felt faint. She saw him at the kitchen table, leaning over his newspaper, looking up suddenly, red suspenders taut over his shoulders, the black mustache, the eyes smoldering, something in the paper reminding him of insult. "My God," she whispered through the quilted gauze over her mouth.

Vera, eyes brimming, breathing open-mouthed in her mask, said, "Don't look anymore, Mama. Don't look."

Emily was unable to explain that evening what she had seen. It would have been difficult anyway, with Walter and the children and Vera at table, while Nikola boiled potatoes and heated the stuffed cabbage he'd made two days ago, telling Vera to sit down, he could do this. And Walter told Vera to keep out of the way, though she fidgeted and smacked her lips with disapproval.

"This is too acidic." David, a tall melancholic boy renowned for high scores in math, pushed a sliver of green pepper aside with his fork.

Phoebe giggled, squirming in her seat, her blonde, woolly hair at constant odds with any attempt to tame it. "I'm an older sister now, Grandma."

"I know, sweetie."

"I'm going to teach Shirley Ann how to read." Phoebe leaped from her seat, to get the schoolbook she'd brought with her, but Vera seized her arm and said, "No! You're not excused!"

Walter said, "Oh . . . ." and Phoebe, forced into her seat, said, "She'll never read. She'll be stupid!"

"But you don't know anything. What could you teach her?" David said, a smile forming among the shadows of his face. He twitched his head upward, and now the smile was gleaming, and he patted Phoebe on her roused, blonde head.

"Don't touch me, weirdo!"

Walter, half smiling, a kind of genial flush pervading him, tapped her on the back of the head. "Just listen to yourself," he said.

The children were a relief, Emily thought, even though she was annoyed by Walter's history-teacher's manner he used with his own children.

"You. You should eat more," Nikola said, his gruffness surrounding Emily like air warmed to the right temperature. He pushed the plate closer, pointing with his fork, but she pushed it back. "You stuff me like a goose!" she said.

"Okay, okay," Nikola said, raising his eyebrows and his hands.

Walter began rubbing his eyes, going into his stuffed-sinus routine, while Vera wearily said, really, this was too much. It was too much for Emily to be driving down from home. Did she have to worry about her mother at such a time? How much could one person do? Braces for Phoebe. David's upcoming SATs. Her own job for a fuel-oil company about to be cut back. She did not discuss what her mother already knew about the week to come, when Shirley Ann might become irredeemably damaged. The months or years beyond that. The expense. A child that might drag her foot, her face twisted upward from the mouth, her attempts at conversation compromised by a difficulty in maintaining eye contact.

And yet, Emily thought, trapped in such a body could be a person like herself—someone once trapped inside another language.

That night, she lay awake thinking of last things. Nikola had no idea. And she felt a long, slow triste, a blushing sadness, an attachment to things like the Toby jugs she'd been dusting, even the acrostic done in the Sunday paper that she slipped into the bag Nikola would tie with twine and put out with the Monday pickup. Everything she touched lingered on her fingertips. And she accused herself of selfishness. Shirley Ann had to be saved. Called to continuously like someone in a coma. When she closed her eyes, she sensed a great sea, she floated, clouds congealed against a dark sky, and she jolted awake, her legs trembling, as if she'd been falling.

She hadn't expected to hear Nikola moaning. In the darkness she'd heard him but thought it was an echo of her dreaming, of her twilight mood. He moaned again, and she realized the sound was coming from below. She turned on the light, put on her glasses, and found Nikola sprawled on the floor, between their beds, a bump forming on his right temple where the skin had split. "Nikola!" She was so certain it was a stroke that all she could think of was to get him to move his legs. And when he did so, she began to feel relieved. Then she saw the vomit stains on the front of his pajamas. He rolled on his side and began to heave. Nothing came.

She questioned him as he lay on the floor, now opening his eyes, now grimacing. He sat up. He'd gotten up two or three times, he said, purging himself in the bathroom, but he'd come back this time and . . . he must have fainted and hit his head. There. He pointed to a sharp corner of the French Provincial end table. The peppers, he said, something in the peppers. Did she feel okay? Emily was confused. She so rarely thought of anything happening to him. She managed to get out of bed and bring back a glass of water. He sat on the edge of the bed and drank slowly. She said, "You see the doctor in the morning!"

He put the glass on her table, near the Millay book, on the very spot where the garnet had last appeared. "Why? What's he going to do?"

He clasped his large, freckled hands between his knees, his slippered feet an inch from the floor. With his head bowed, the wattles at his throat seemed more pronounced. And through his thinning hair, once a nearly Titian red, she could discern other freckles, brown sunspots that might turn a raspberry red on a scalp already treated for epitheliomas. She felt a sudden chill, a lightness in her arms and legs, and thought what would happen now, if she fainted?

Nikola told her to go back to sleep. His stomach had emptied out. Nothing more could happen. As she lay back under the blankets, heat seemed to re-enter her limbs. She half expected the garnet to appear, and, face on pillow, peeked at the table and studied what had become its accustomed spot. Nothing. But within seconds she was dreaming of her mother seated on the old sofa, its bright twists of lilies and irises imprinted on black fabric. Was it the apartment in Astoria? Her mother was like a figure in a garden, glowing, her long hair braided and pulled up to the crown of her head, where a white bow disappeared into the light that emanated from a source behind the sofa. It seemed so commercial, she thought. So false. Yet her mother was smiling, cheeks bright, her eyes with their nearly Asian slope and the old amused look, as when Emily would come home from school with A's in everything except math.

My mother looks happy, she thought. Then the girl in the white dress rushed up and, kneeling, put her head in the woman's lap. It could have been a scene from one of the Cassatt pictures Emily had hung in the living room, counterpointing ceramic bluebirds on shelves opposite. It could have been herself, home from first communion.

That morning, she found an emerald on her night table. And this time, Nikola saw it. He held it to the light, turned it over in his palm, shook his head. "It's happening again?" he asked.

"It's nothing," she said.

Wilted from the night's viral attack, he sat on the bed, poking the emerald with his finger. "My God," he said.

"Put it back on the table. It'll probably be gone by afternoon."

"Is something bad going to happen?" He looked very pale.

"I don't know," she said.

"It's Shirley Ann, isn't it? That poor little baby." He put the emerald back on Emily's table, and lay down, staring at the ceiling. That he took the appearances of the stones as a matter of course continued to surprise her. This thing was nothing but a weakness in her identity. It wasn't even compassion. Things flowed through her as through a vessel, leaving her empty. Fatigued. But Nikola would argue that the stones proved something else. What, he couldn't explain. And he left it at that. A mystery.

But the emerald did not disappear. A day later, with Nikola able to take solid food, color restored to his face, and with Emily fighting off an anger that her daughter Vera had thrust a dying child upon her—when she herself had so little time—the little emerald reflected the sunlight from its facets next to the

Millay book and the clock. She covered it with a tissue. It would be soon, her death.

Vera called that afternoon. "This week is the critical one," she said. "Maybe it's better if she just died." She said Walter was trying to keep her spirits up. But Phoebe was having trouble in school. The teachers were talking about an attention-span deficiency. David was off on his own. She couldn't talk to him. He fought with her about every little thing. "They'll know after a week. They'll know if she's damaged."

"Maybe it would be better," Emily said. "If she died."

For the rest of that week, she made lists as she gathered the papers and account books and policies that Nikola would have to deal with. She wrote out pages of instructions that she knew Vera would read aloud to him. At night, she dreamt of colored mists, sometimes yellow, sometimes blue, or smoke-colored shapes like demons, and she would wake afraid, drenched in sweat, unable to call to Nikola because he would only be frightened himself. What could he do? She thought of him alone in the living room, watching TV, his eyes glazed. She thought of her chair by the yellow lamp, where she did her acrostics. In her mind, she walked through all the rooms vacated of her presence. She didn't know if her grief was for Nikola or for herself. She didn't know if it was wrong of her to not tell him she was dying. Her mother appeared again, this time haggard, the way she was when they lived in Astoria, Emily's father coming home unpleasant, scoffing at the food. She dreamt of her friends in the third grade: fat Stefanie with the braids; Aurora with the eyeglasses, the girl she sold her pencil box to when her father withheld money for a trip to the museum. She felt a terrible gripe in her abdomen, remembering Vera's birth. That wet, slippery child held to the light.

She thought of Shirley Ann. The whiteness sliding past. She breathed in an air rich with oxygen, feeling pain in her sternum, as if she'd swallowed an icy cold drink. Again, she dreamt of the girl in white dress dancing in and out of the wagon wheel spokes.

"Emily. Wake up." It was Nikola. "Vera's on the phone."

She trembled. In this moment, she thought she was midway. A great lightness, a giddy freedom, had altered the gravity of her body's center. She floated away from voices she had been so intent on hearing only yesterday, like her mother's, while in the same dream her father had turned away, chin lowered to his chest, dejected and seated in the chair where she did her acrostics. In this very moment, Nikola handed her the phone. She panicked. "No!" she said. "No! Take it away!" It was too painful. She couldn't do it.

"Emily. It's Vera." He told her to put on her glasses, though he knew she never wore glasses when talking on the phone. It was her habit to talk with eyes closed, as if shrinking the distance between herself and auditor, as if the intimacy of that darkness defied time and space even more than the electronics of telephone equipment. He said it anyway, hoping to break her out of her mood. He did it on instinct. "Put on your glasses, Emily!"

"Niko, I can't help it!" She fumbled for her glasses and brushed aside the tissue that had been covering the emerald. The stone had disappeared. Was she being called? Had the calling ceased? She could smell the electrical odor again, even though Nikola had removed the narcissi two days ago. Her hand twitched away from the clock, the lamp, anything with current. The odor seemed to emanate from the phone and she began to weep, taking it from Nikola, feeling helpless, brutalized.

"Mama, I know you'll think I'm crazy. I'm sorry to wake you. Mama, I've been talking with a woman here at the hospital. Her husband's in a coma from a car accident. You know what she does? She prays. And she has her friends praying too. She says today he actually opened his eyes. I asked Walter and the children. They said they'd do it. But I don't trust them. Mama, would you pray for Shirley Ann? I think she's going to die, Mama. I think I'm going to die." She started sobbing in the way Emily had not heard since Vera's childhood, a deep thrusting from the lungs, a terrible moaning.

Nikola took the phone. "What's the matter? What's happening? Your mother is not feeling well. Is Walter there?"

Vera told him that Walter was home with the children. She was sitting in the downstairs waiting room at the hospital, watching TV talk shows, listening to the woman whose husband was in a coma. She couldn't help it. She was sorry. Was something wrong with mother?

"Now," Nikola said, moving his hand up and down, "now, you calm yourself." He told her Emily was probably getting what he had the other night. A virus. He sounded just like the Indian doctor they used to have at the HMO. Everything was attributed to a virus. "A viroos." By the time Emily was willing to speak, Nikola waved her off.

"Let me speak to my daughter!" she demanded hoarsely. It was too late. He'd hung up. She should get some rest. He went into his rational mode. Without rest, he said, you couldn't think. You couldn't do anything.

She was furious. "You don't do that!" she said. "You don't cut me off like that!" He tried to soothe her. Did she want some water?

"I don't want a damn thing from you!" she said. "You can go to hell!"

"Where do you think I am!" he shouted. "I am in hell!"

She pulled the blanket up to her chin. Would anyone pray for *her,* if no one knew what was happening? "Go back to bed," she said.

"Uh!" Nikola removed his slippers.

She heard them hit the floor with a soft *flapflop.* It was a familiar sound. Soothing.

"Do you want something?" he said.

"Go to sleep." She knew he would drift off. She understood that the emerald had disappeared because she no longer needed her attention drawn that way. Now she couldn't think of anything else. And Shirley Ann. She couldn't help. She began to think of Shirley Ann as someone else's baby, a spirit gone astray, seeking a material soul—come from as far away as Kamenica, where her father had been born, where women in black dresses and black kerchiefs carried loads of firewood on their backs, pressing themselves against stone walls as trucks spluttered past. A baby with its mother lost, not dead. And it had found its own way to a door that opened like a wound. And here it was, slipped forth as Shirley Ann. Damaged coming through the wrong portal and too soon.

She dreamt of the girl in white dress. There was no one else. It seemed the same polished wood floor in the same room, but with furniture changed to resemble a living room or kitchen. It was always the same room. She understood that. She recognized the girl's hair as her own, luxuriant, blonde, hanging in thick, natural curls as they were before her mother had cut them, saying, in America, you should look American. The girl

approached her shyly, swinging her dress back and forth, looking down. It was right, she thought, that the girl should be
alone. And she tried to look beyond, over the girl's head, where
she expected a window radiant with light, a doorway, a trans-
lucence. But there was only the wall. And the girl lifted her
face, eyes blue as her own had been, before they bleared, a flush
of excitement coloring the left cheek. Emily extended her
hand, confused, waiting to be led away, though there seemed
no way out. She comforted herself that Nikola would understand their last fight had not been real. It was not the sum of
their life. It was nothing. She began to weep, lowering her
hand, then raising it again.

"Why are you doing that?" the girl said.

"Because I'm ready now," Emily said.

"Ready for what?"

"For you to take me away. We'll be together again."

"But we are, now, silly." The girl danced round and round.
Emily began to sob.

"Don't do that. It's all right. It's me, Grandma. It's Shirley
Ann." And she held her hand up, waiting for Emily to take it.
"You have to take me with *you*. There." The girl pointed to an
area that Emily had never been able to turn around to inspect.
"There, Grandma."

They saw Nikola, head in hands, sitting on the edge of his
bed.

ꙂESCENDING FIRE

1993

Alan lay on his stomach dimly aware of Norma's needles implanted like Lilliputian fenceposts along each side of his spine. His forehead and chin were pressed into a face-shaped frame that was covered with foam rubber and jutted out from the edge of the table. He opened his eyes and stared down at the ocher designs in Norma's Navajo rug and inhaled the sweet incense burning near the door, opposite the small lavatory she had installed in the solar room used for her practice. A small ceramic heater blew warmly. A network of branches from a gnarled magnolia tree reached over the glass roof of the room. Earlier, on his back, he'd been staring at the bare branches, vaguely aware that two hours ago he had been counseling his own clients at the Agency. And that for several months, his father had been visiting him in the basement, sometimes swinging on a meat hook; sometimes seated nude upon a swing, chest and pubic hair all gray, his penis small as a baby's. Lisa, who'd almost lost her father to a heart attack the year before, had said, "No, I don't need to see him. It's okay. But don't do anything weird." She'd gone back to her murder mystery, the quilt floating loosely over her in their king-size bed, while the house, their very first, creaked and whispered in the change of seasons. A thermometer in its scabbard lay in the recess of the headboard. And the testing kit with a + and − window lay on the white shelf in the bathroom.

"Are you comfortable?" Norma bent over him, eyes dark and glowing, and pressed lightly into his back. "I'm just waiting until the redness disappears."

He lifted his face out of the mask. "Yes," he said. "But my feet are a little cold."

"How's that?" She folded a blanket over the soles of his feet. She had nimble hands and seemed to float about the table. If he were upright, in ballet slippers, he'd be on point.

He wiggled his toes to prevent a cramp, and he remembered how his sister would yell at him for touching her dancing shoes. And his father would say in the kitchen, "It's not right for a boy. That's all I know." Esther, her dark face narrow and pinched, saying, "Don't touch my things. Just because you're their son doesn't mean you can do whatever you want." Crushing beneath her heel the little father and mother figures from her dollhouse, snapping off their arms and legs, because he had been playing with them. "I told you," she hissed, "I told you." Years later, talking with Lisa about Esther's son Edwin, he said, "It was as if her anger attacked the fetus."

The faces of his clients drifted into his mind. There was Elizabeth Kuhl, writing poems filled with a young girl's romantic dreams, though she was over thirty and had two children—unaware what she felt about a father who had shot a judge, and then himself. There was Jabar, contrasting himself with a cousin who lived in the Bronx. "He don't use drugs. He don't rob nobody. He just steals cars. He got shot right here." He placed the tip of his index finger between his eyebrows, the scowl for a moment gone from his broad dark face. "But I didn't need no bullet to know where I was at. That's why the angel come to me."

Alan's mouth suddenly filled with saliva.

He'd always had trouble with his sister. He'd always tried to learn how she lived, what she did, why she was the way she was. He'd be caught fooling with her things, her tapes, records. And always she came down on him. Maybe the anger had something to do with their grandmother—their mother's mother—coming to live with them in the Bronx. Maybe it had to do with their father losing his business and going to work in the deli department of a Waldbaum's, where he hailed the mothers and the old women and the children—always needing a haircut, the hair growing down the back of his neck. Whenever Esther thought she could get some attention, something happened. Like Grandma moving in—a woman who in her better days could have been a second mother, but now she was old and ill and smelled bad. Grandma's return meant the telling again of the stories of escape from Rumania, how Abram the only son, Esther and Alan's only maternal uncle, had not escaped. Their mother would cry, trying to console her own mother, who seemed to be reliving it all. And Alan wondered if his mother had ever felt angry the way Grandma talked about Abram—as if she and her three sisters didn't count. And that anger was passed on, seeping into Esther's soul.

"Are you afraid," Lisa had asked, "we'll have a defective child?"

"I don't think so," he'd said, though he remembered the disappointment, the weeping in his mother's kitchen, when Esther's first son was born with Down syndrome.

Less than two months after the headstone ceremony, his father had visited him in the basement. "What's to be afraid of?" he said. Spread-eagle, hanging from four separate ropes tied to his wrists and ankles, he looked like a skydiver free-falling toward earth.

Norma leaned over. "Everything's gone into your head."

"I know," Alan said. It was hard to talk with his face pressing into the mask.

"We call it rising heart-fire," she said, tilting her head to one side, smiling.

He wondered if she and her physician husband disagreed on diagnoses. He often saw the man watering the garden, talking to their dog, a German shepherd with a deep menacing growl that disappeared once a person was in the house or Norma's solar office. He wondered what his supervisor, Ruth, would say if he told her that his clients' *chi* was too weak; their energy bodies were fading. Their heart-fire was escaping from the pleural cavity into the head, and feelings that belonged in the center of being had become a kind of mechanical heat driving an obsessive engine up above, which is why he'd been gnawing his lower lip, making raw the inside of his cheeks, little white spots appearing on his gums.

"It's not helping that your father is hanging around," Lisa had said. She'd been coming home tired from her make-do job at the lighting-fixture store in Bedford Hills, near the end of the local strip, just beyond a McDonald's and two auto dealerships with pennants and revolving logos. It was her second change of jobs since leaving a small, weekly newspaper, but at least she wasn't commuting to Manhattan.

Alan had discarded the theory of hallucinations when Lisa found things under her in bed, bits of brittle amber-like peas that she said were bruising her legs. But they disappeared, and on the next visit his father said, "It's a way of saying hello."

"Is this a haunting?" Alan asked. His mother had insisted that he and Esther take some of the insurance money. He was worried it had cursed the house.

"You shouldn't have bought on low ground," his father said.

"Don't change the subject," Alan said.

"There is only one subject!"

"Do you do this to mother? Or Esther?" He imagined his sister, her flushed cheeks, her hectic body movements, her finger pointing. *"You? No. No way. Forget it!"*

"We talk, your mother and me," his father said, rotating slowly on the rope that was tied under his armpits. "But not through the mouth. Through the mind. She is getting to be a nice old lady."

"Is there something you need from me?"

"Need?" his father replied. "I don't have needs."

Norma twisted the needles. "The redness is almost gone. How are you feeling?"

"Uuuh!" he grunted affirmatively. It was the kind of sound that Jabar had emitted when Alan asked if he believed that an angel had actually come to visit him. In constant trouble with the police, Jabar was put on probation in Lincoln Hall, where he then spent almost every night for a year drunk in his room, until an angel appeared and told him to straighten out. "I wasn't surprised," he said. "I knew something real bad or real good was goin' to happen."

"You're very tight here," Norma said, pressing gently against the muscles that ran along each side of his neck. "It's like the abdomen. Attacked by thought."

He looked down at the design in the rug. It reminded him of a sweater Lisa used to wear, its bright orange and ocher like a contained fire out of which her face emerged narrow and beautiful. He wondered if they shouldn't have stayed in their apartment in Yonkers, the little weigelia-covered terrace overlooking the Cross County Parkway that arched over the sunken, tire-shredded corridors of the Thruway. And in the distance, on the other side of the Parkway and the traffic, arose the high ground of Seminary Avenue, where the gold-leafed dome of St. Joseph's Seminary glittered in the sunset.

He was adrift on a field of gold when he heard Norma's voice.

"Are you comfortable?"

"Uhhh," he replied, then unstuck his face briefly, and lowered himself back into the mask. Was sudden death worse than suicide? He thought of Elizabeth Kuhl's father, the desperation that had driven him. He had discussed that with his father who had been rotating from a rope tied to the cold water pipe. The house—in bosky northern Westchester where several reservoirs stored drinking water for New York City—had been vacated by a woman whose husband had fled to Florida without her. It had plumbing problems and a cracked floor from an underground stream, but that was why it had been affordable. The driveway sloped down from a road that ran along the Amawalk Reservoir. At the end of the reservoir, to the east, was Lincoln Hall, a school for troubled boys like Jabar, where Alan did volunteer work when he wasn't working at the Agency. The proximity of Lincoln Hall, from which an occasional boy would escape to maraud and loot the surrounding homes, had also made the house affordable. One year, two white youths from the Hall had murdered an old woman on Primrose Road and beaten her husband.

"I told you," his father had said, turning slowly, "it's not what you're doing *at* the end that counts. It's what you were doing all the years *before* the end." He grunted and shivered, rubbing his hands up and down his arms. "You know how damp it is down here?"

"What I don't understand," Alan said, "is why you went to Atlanta."

"It wasn't Atlanta," his father replied. He was dressed as if going to work at his old deli at the end of Bronx River Road, in Yonkers, wearing a short-sleeved white shirt and loose chinos, and over that his white apron with pockets filled with peppermint candies he had sucked on after he quit smoking. He still wore the kind of clumsy orthopedic shoes his Uncle Victor had used. "Bad feet run in the family," he'd said. "And bad luck."

"Okay," Alan said, "not Atlanta. Marietta."

"That they say May-retta," his father corrected, wagging his finger. It was the sort of niggling that had made conversation difficult when he was alive.

"Why didn't you stay up here? You could be living in Heritage Hills, right down the road from me."

"You think I wouldn't still have a bad heart?" He seemed interested, and slowly rotated away from his son, toward the wall, and then came round again.

"I think you should have talked more about it, before you moved," Alan said.

His father shook his head. "You know what I think?" he said. "I think you're still jealous we moved close to your sister."

"You're wrong," Alan said.

"In a few minutes," Norma said, "I'll take your pulses. Then we'll try some things along your wrists. And your pinkies."

He tried to nod. He caught himself chewing his lower lip again, and when he tried to halt that, realized that his tongue was trembling in his mouth. Then, just as suddenly, it stopped. He turned over and felt the blood shifting in his face, his head. His lower sinuses opened like a window, and he breathed freely.

He had been amazed the other night, coming upstairs after a chat with his father, to find Lisa awake, reading.

"Am I catching this from you?" she asked.

"What?"

"When was the last time you slept normally?" She put the book down and turned over on her side facing him. She looked tired.

"Probably when I was nine years old," he said.

Two nights ago, she had said everything seemed out of control, who to invite to the house, who not, his mother, his Aunt Sarah, his sister and the children. She complained that lately they both seemed too tired. The book she was reading— a collection of poems by an author known as Danielle, who pretended to travel through time with her lover—lay pages-down on her stomach. He read the blurb on the back cover that praised the metaphors.

"Maybe we're dysfunctional," she said.

"I thought you didn't like those terms."

"Well, maybe there are times it's the right term."

"You think my sperm are swimming the wrong way?"

He thought about the time she was covering a story in Washington, taking a cab to Union Station, disputing with the driver the cost for luggage, until the driver seized her by the throat. "American bitch!" He thought about the things that his mother, before their marriage, had censured in her:

jogging in shorts that showed pale crescents of rear end, her jeans and cotton tops from India that bled in the wash. And he thought of his mother walking down the supermarket aisles in Marietta, her small upper body sunken into her hips as she walked and rolled like a sailor.

"I love you," he said.

"Maybe," she said. She turned away from him and returned to her book.

"I really do," he said.

"You just don't like to touch me anymore."

"That's not true!"

Norma held his limp wrist and took his pulse in two different areas, then moved around the table and did the other wrist. "Better," she said. "But you're still racing a bit on the right side."

"I guess I'm thinking too much," he said. He lay back and stared upward at the overhanging tree's interlacing branches, the divided light, the cooling brightness of the late afternoon.

"I'll ask you to take a deep breath," Norma said. "Then, when you let it out, you'll feel a little something at the edge of your pinky."

"Fire away," he said.

He was thinking about Elizabeth Kuhl, who had appeared at her last session with scrapes on her elbow, signs of recent injuries on her forehead and right cheek that displayed small scabs. She had fallen from her bike, she said. Then the energy seemed to leap from her, as she talked about her writing. His efforts to get her to write about something rooted in real experiences, like her father's death, had fallen upon an inattention, an abrupt immobility in her features, a dimming of her eyes, as in someone being lied to.

"Breathe in," Norma said.

He did. Then he breathed out and felt a pinprick in his pinky. He remembered Lisa complaining about her employer, Jeff Metzger, at the lamp store. Jeff was going through a divorce. "We were doing inventory, counting halogen bulbs, bending down to avoid the hanging fixtures, and he brushed against me."

"Was he touching you? I mean, really touching?"

"He was going to."

"Like this?"

Afterwards, they went downstairs, and standing in their robes on the outside landing, in the mild March evening, discussed what kind of fixture to put above the door. He wanted a hanging globe, she something like a lantern, to go with the wrought-iron railing. She quoted her father on something electrical, and he countered with something about roundness. A globe. She leaned into him and said she didn't really care. She quoted one of Danielle's poems:

> I arose in light gentle, a sleeper
> wistful and weeping in her empty room.
> Where we met, no marigold or aster
> lingered. When you touched me, all of time bloomed.

He felt the entire softness of her body, and they went inside and made love on the stairs.

"Breathe in," Norma said. "Now out."

He felt something sharp again enter his pinky, and he listened to the *plipping* of the little three-tiered fountain Norma had just installed; a bowl brimmed with water that then spilled into a bowl below.

He wondered why, the other night, when he'd given his father a glass of water, the glass hadn't passed through his father's hand. "How come I can't touch you?"—he tried, but his hand went through his father's swinging legs—"but you can hold things like this glass?"

"Only protoplasm goes through. Anything living goes right through me."

"You make me sound like a virus."

"A famous writer once said life was a disease. Not normal in the universe."

He felt his hand and forearm relax, and he wished that Elizabeth were being visited by her father, who she could not imagine past the time she was twelve years old. He thought about Jabar. He tried to imagine the angel as Jabar had described him, a tall thin naked African with a gold chain around his waist.

"Same time next week?" Norma asked. She sat at her desk with the appointment book on her lap.

"Yes, yes," he said.

"I have some herbs I want you to try. To make a decoction."

"Sure," he said.

"And these." She held up a baggie filled with gray caplets that smelled like parsley. The herbs in a paper bag looked like corn husks and bits of cork and scrapings of root.

That evening, he boiled the herbs in a saucepan, and the liquid turned tawny and gave off an acrid odor. Lisa leaned over his shoulder. "It smells like a swamp." He let it cool and then poured some into a glass. She laughed after he swished some of it in his mouth. He smiled, and she laughed louder.

His teeth had turned yellow.

When his mother called, he argued with her over when he and Lisa could visit Marietta. Then Lisa's parents had him and Lisa over for dinner, and he toured his father-in-law's new workshop, the converted garage where ever since he'd gone on disability from his heart attack, he worked on a stained-glass window he called *The Daughters of Lazarus,* showing Alan his drawings, the cartoon for the window: a great long sheet of white paper on which were drawn two women and a man rising from the ground. The women were Lisa and her sister. The heart, he said, was like a rubber ball that when you squeeze it returns to its shape. His wouldn't do that anymore. Once squeezed, it remained shriveled like a prune. He demonstrated by opening and closing his fist, and Alan could see in him Lisa's love of detail. He watched his father-in-law's perfect teeth click shut in a smile, the man's heart trouble evident only in the terribly slow manner of his speech, the patient deliberateness of his reaching for a tool. Alan wondered if he still made love.

When he and Lisa returned home, his mother called back. "Esther's leaving the boys with me, and Sarah's helping out. So maybe, June is not a good time for you and Lisa to come down. I don't have room, with the boys."

It would mean staying with Aunt Sarah, her tall narrow house, three bedrooms in a row upstairs, the guests using the downstairs bathroom. "Why is she leaving the boys with you?"

"She's worn out. It's the only time Chip can get away."

He remembered Esther returning home from college, her record scarred with incompletes, just as he was entering the Bronx High School of Science. She took a job in Wanamaker's in the Cross County Shopping Center, opposite where he and Lisa would later live, not far fron the little shopping center

where their father had gone bankrupt with the deli. In Wanamaker's, Esther was working the men's department and met
Chip Goldberg, a chiropractor with startled green eyes. He had
just gotten divorced. She helped him find a dress shirt 40%
cotton with 16 neck, 32 sleeve. She no longer seemed angry.
They got married. Then Edwin was born, and the anger returned.

"Well, I don't know if we can get down later. It's too hot
later."

"You can stay in air-conditioning."

"I don't think Esther has the right to do this. To you."

"What else do I do down here, me and Sarah?" Her other
sisters were in a facility that allowed them their own apartment, and across the hall, through swinging doors, was the
annex they would live in when no longer ambulatory. "The real
exit," Sarah said. The sisters in the facility had grown so close
in their daily routines, playing Scrabble, watching soaps, taking naps, that the other two sisters were like strangers. "When
Rachel goes," Sarah said, "Eve won't last a month." Their
children, in Ohio, Colorado, and California, visited once a
year.

He remembered crying when Esther had held out his dead
turtle, the one he'd insisted was alive, that was stinking up his
room. She'd almost been sympathetic. "See," she said, poking
its limp head with a pencil, "it probably died of old age." And
she'd kissed him on the cheek, the way years later she would
kiss Edwin, when he hurt his lip falling down.

After Lisa fell asleep reading Danielle, he prowled in the
kitchen, the air heavy with the scent of his herbal decoction.
He ate an apple. He flipped through channels on the TV,
muting the sound, the room flickering in glare. Then he went

back upstairs, to the bedroom. Lisa had thrown off the covers, one leg drawn up shining white, her other leg straight. A great warmth flooded him and he removed his pajamas and lay next to her, and stroked her until she awakened, murmuring. He slid down, he was at her breast, his hand deep between her legs, he spoke her name over and over. She groaned and took him inside her. And he flowed forth. He died.

But he couldn't sleep. With Lisa breathing softly, he went down into the kitchen, and began writing on the right-hand side of a yellow pad:

> 1. Insomnia is seeing a car about to swerve and hit a man and not telling the man but always seeing the car swerve.

He remembered saying to his father the other night, "Leave me alone." "You still don't get it," his father said. "You still think, compartment A, compartment B. Everything has two ends, like a tunnel. Entrances, exits, it doesn't matter, the same thing, forward, backward. It is like a child drawing a line with a pencil toward the end of a page. If I take away the end of the page, which way is the pencil moving? Like the time you wrote your mother that you didn't want to see Esther anymore because she was always mad at you—then her baby gets born with this thing wrong with him, and you can't figure out if not seeing Esther is also saying something about her little boy. And you know your mother is crying every night. And whatever Esther did to you was done to a person no longer there except in your mind. And if you forget everything but the love that should be in your heart—tell me. Which way is your pencil moving?"

2. Insomnia is not distinct from the moral sense. Being awake itself a kind of action. But the original action or lack of it, the moral thing, can never be accessed = it is not a palpable action, so there is no issue of ethics. But if I had *not* done something right, the not doing would still constitute an action, in this case negated to the point of being not nonaction but action subsequently subtracted. So: an action did first occur. Then it was not erased—because if it was erased, there would be no problem, everything back to null—it was neutralized. Therefore implicitly there even when not because the act of negation could not occur w/o the prior act it had its effects upon. If this were not so we would have effects w/o causes. No durations but incessantly original unconnected moments.

3. Something sexual. The body in aloneness. Wanting.

4. The luminous numbers of the alarm clock shining through my eyelids.

5. Too little use during the day of my being which continues to run like an engine during the night until the fuel is consumed.

(Dear Lisa: there are feelings I never tell you about. Beautiful feelings. The way you are beautiful.)

He wondered how cold he must have seemed when Elizabeth Kuhl confided that she'd slept with her husband's best friend.

"Is this terribly wrong?" she'd asked, her face showing small areas of pink where the scabs from her accident had been. "Well," he'd said. And then he'd followed the usual course. Getting her to say what she felt about it. Did *she* feel it was right or wrong? Here he was trying to get her to talk about her father—an obsessed man who, when a court case went against him, had murdered the arbiter and killed himself—and she was jumping into bed with another man.

Wrong? The judgment itself arose like so much else out of how one viewed the past. He remembered that Jabar—hidden deep within a shirt and sweater and many-zippered jacket, smelling unwashed and rank—had confessed that he was getting worried. His angel had only visited once, and within a few months he had to decide where to go. Back to the Bronx, or to the other school, in Rockland County, where he could live while he took courses at the community college—a place where Alan taught an introductory psych course in the morning, before he went to work at the Agency. "I'm a leader, I know that," Jabar said, his face shiny with sweat, his eyes bright and focused. "But I've been a negative leader. Now I'm a positive leader. I mean, I don't want to go around hurting people. I used to beat people up, with my friends. We didn't care, man. We didn't. And I could see that when I first came here. You thought I would hurt you or something. You were afraid. I used to like that." "And now?" Alan asked. He was disappointed that he'd not been able to conceal his feelings, remembering how he'd read Jabar's scowl, mistaking it for anger, when it was the same expression he'd seen lately on his father's face, when he asked him how long they would go on, the visits, the midnight drinks of water, the stories that led nowhere.

Norma was palpating each side of his jaw. "I'm just going to put one here, and here," she said, indicating an area just below the jaw muscles.

In bed, Lisa had asked him, "Do you think I should quit my job? It's so meaningless. Showing women lamps. Talking about what goes with what." "I thought you wanted to get away from the other stuff." "Well, I was disgusted with the violence." "Maybe you're around abused women too much." She had been attending meetings in Bedford on Wednesday evenings, after work, working on a series of articles on the wives of policemen, interviewing inmates at the Bedford Women's Prison. "I don't know." She lay back and stared at the ceiling. "I mean, who really gives a shit anyway?" Within minutes she had fallen asleep, and downstairs, his father, looking very comfortable in a blue polyester suit, had said, "You know, you're a very nice man. You were always a nice kid. Always polite. I worry that maybe you need to be more of a sonuvabitch."

"Do you feel a tightness here?" Norma asked. She pressed the tips of her fingers into the area just below his sternum. "Here?"

"Yes," he said. "It feels bruised."

"You should try breathing from down there," she said. "From your diaphragm. Down here"—she moved her hand down just below his navel—"is one of the paths of fire when it's in flight.

"Breathe in. Now out." She inserted the needle and rotated it. He felt a narrow column of heat twisting within his jaw like a tiny whirlwind.

He had decided to be firm. To have a showdown. He had

allowed his father to ramble, like a client, like Alice, the retiring nurse awaiting her first pension check, convinced she would die before it came; Alice, who talked loosely about the past, the new bagel store in the Spring Valley Center, about the Haitian cabdrivers driving like the Hasids from New Square, reckless and foreign; her closely cut gray hair giving her the look of someone going into combat.

"If he were alive, would we want him living with us?" Lisa had said, pointing to the floor and the basement beneath it. "I can't even go down there to do the laundry."

It seemed unfair.

Norma leaned over him, swabbing with alcohol two parallel areas high on his forehead and implanting her needles. They were, he realized, the same places that Michelangelo had sculpted horns on the head of Moses. She had already inserted needles at each end of his jaw. And one just below his right knee, and one in the middle of each palm. A heavy rain the night before had washed the blown magnolia blooms down onto the glass roof, where they formed a pale scarlet-and-brown mosaic. When he looked up, with the bloom-splattered glass above her, her small, finely featured face framed by dark hair, her hands raised, Norma was like an angel in a stained-glass window.

Jabar had been excited, pushing back his peaked, gold-braided cap, looking behind him as he spoke, his stoic demeanor and gloomy patience swept away. "I saw him!"

"But why would he be here?" Before he'd left the house, Lisa had come in from the bathroom, holding up the kit. "Another minus." And as he held her, she'd sighed just like his supervisor, Ruth.

"It was him, it was the angel. He was driving a Toyota, and

he pulled up in front of the laundromat, and a woman came out with a basket of clothes, and he drove off with her. Man!" Jabar had come to the Agency in Spring Valley, after touring the school he might transfer to.

"He was driving a car? Isn't that strange?"

"Naw, naw. That's the way he is, the way he comes to you. He takes on your lifestyle. When I lived in the Bronx, near Yankee Stadium, he would've been a dealer or one of those guys outside the Stadium selling programs." He went on to describe his old neighborhood, how he'd left to live with his father who had taken up with a Haitian woman in Nyack. How he got on probation. How he'd been drinking in his room at the school, until the angel came to him.

Alan realized that where Jabar lived was only blocks from where his father's Uncle Victor had once disappeared in 1959, before he made it big in the early '60s with a line of frozen make-your-own sundaes. "How do you feel about that? About the angel not coming to you, and then you see him?"

"I'm really glad for her, for that woman. I mean, the angel gives you what you need, what's right for you. This woman didn't have no car. I could tell she probably had a job and kids. And no man. Her man probably left her. Because he couldn't be responsible. The angel teaches you that. To be responsible. To be positive."

For the rest of the forty-five minutes, Jabar talked rapidly about getting a diploma. Becoming a counselor. When he opened the door to leave, he froze. "There he is!"

Alan looked out and saw Junior Davidson, a tall thin man who did maintenance work for the building that housed the Agency. He was on his knees, at the water cooler, adjusting something on the pipe that led to the wall. Junior looked up at the incredulous Jabar and stared blankly. Alan knew that Junior was friendly with counselors at school, that they hired him for odd jobs.

Jabar walked up and touched Junior on the shoulder. "Hey, man. Aw, shit! Aw, shit, man!"

Alan took Jabar back inside, and they talked about what difference it made, whether the angel was real or not. Jabar kept striking his knees with his open palms, standing up and sitting down, looking at the wall.

"It doesn't mean they don't want the best for you," Alan said. He was trying to convince Jabar that he himself hadn't been in on it.

"They shouldn't made me a damn fool," Jabar said.

"Everything you've been saying is still true," Alan said. "Everything you want for yourself is still valid." What difference did it make, after all, if an angel were real? Something continued. Something unfolded itself.

"They shouldn't taken away my pride." Jabar's head was bowed, and he clasped his hands between his knees.

Later that day, Elizabeth Kuhl entered his office and flung herself into the chair. She leaned forward with her scrubbed, shiny, finely sculpted face, and said, "Just tell me. I only want to know. Do you have any feelings for me?"

Norma's fingers explored the top of his skull, moving down to the tightness of his temples. For a moment, he thought he was with Lisa.

"This can't go on," Lisa had said, and he'd thought she meant her job, the appearance of Jeff's girlfriend, a blonde with two children who visited every day. Or the problem of her article on the abused wives of policemen that had appeared in the local paper. Some of the wives had written to the editor, saying their husbands had never raised a hand to them. They threatened lawsuits.

"It feels very cool there," he said suddenly. The fountain dribbled and plipped, and he thought about the time one of his uncles at a seder had talked about the sons of Aaron, killed by the Lord's descending fire for worshiping false gods. He caught his breath in a semi-sob, then breathed in.

Breathed out.

He had, he thought, been firm. He'd gone into the basement to find his father completely concealed and zipped into a black body bag that had been lowered down on the rope so that it was directly opposite him. He tried to touch it, but his hand went through.

His father's voice was slightly muffled. "Don't worry," he said. "Breathing is not a problem."

"Is this goodbye?"

"Everything is relative," his father said. "Sometimes I feel like something caught in the wing feathers of a bird, I'm a tiny little louse. This bird is soaring over ice mountains, then the bird plunges into the sea and he's flapping there very slowly, underwater, like a puffin. Then he breaks up out of the water. I'm holding on. Everything is a blur."

"You know why I think you're here all the time, talking?"

"Why, Mr. Counselor?"

"I think you're afraid."

He was silent, and Alan could hear him breathing in the body bag. "I'm not afraid," he said.

At dinner, Lisa's mother talked about how well Lisa's sister was doing, setting up computer programs for medical groups. Lisa's father was withdrawn, and Alan thought he wasn't feel-

ing well. Then they went out to his workshop, where a nearly
blind Siamese cat followed him around, mewing incessantly.
They saw the completed cartoon for *The Daughters of Lazarus.*
It was clear now that Lazarus was Lisa's father: dark circles
around the eyes; tight, curly hair; the arm uplifted, ready to
fall around one's shoulders in greeting, though here, drawn on
the paper with a black felt pen, it was a gesture of surprise, as if
to shield his eyes from sudden light. If there was a Christ
raising him from the dead, that figure was not in the frame.
Instead were the daughters: Lisa, her arms raised in a mannered
saint's style; Alexandra, her sister, her long hair twisted around
her neck, looking heavenward. Then his father-in-law showed
Alan the various types of glass he would use, the antique,
pitted, clear glass, the burgundy reds, the vivid greens that
would slash across the father and daughters like divine inter-
vention. And he kept saying, "Great, isn't it? Isn't it great?"
And cool as the workshop was, he'd begun to perspire.

"To tell you the truth," Alan said later in bed, "I was
uncomfortable."

"You're like that a lot," Lisa said, on her side, staring at
him, then reaching out to touch his cheek.

"What?"

"You just don't seem to be inside yourself anymore."

They made love, and he sweated profusely and blamed the
wine.

"Breathe in." Norma was working on his right hand.

He tried to suck air into the pit of his being.

"Now out."

The needle went in, and he nearly whimpered. He remembered last fall, when Esther had visited in Yonkers with the
boys. Edwin suddenly loud, crying, exaggerating the puffy

look of his face that would become more prominent as he got older, and the grin that widened as he threw his head back and looked at something above, enjoying the sensation of his head being back almost on his shoulders. Lisa swept the boy up in her arms and said, "Look, look!" pointing at someone's helium-filled blue and red balloons escaping from the terrace below.

"Just relax now. A few more minutes."

"What does she say?" Lisa asked. "Maybe we should go down."

He was reading the note from his sister. "She says she and Chip are going to Charleston and hope the hurricane didn't destroy everything. She says Chip would love to open a practice down there. Charleston. Savannah. She says she'd hoped to see us."

"Edwin loves being around everyone," Lisa said. "I could see that last time. The way he runs from one person to another, especially Sarah."

"Yeah, well, Esther wonders if he ought to go into a special school."

"I thought Sarah talked her out of that. And your mother."

"I think they're worried about the effect on his brother, of having him around."

"That's a lot of crap and you know it!"

He studied the note. The sun was slanting through the skylight over the breakfast nook, illuminating countless motes. For a minute or two after his vacuuming of the braided rug, he and Lisa had been moving through an eerie colloid of bright particles. It was Saturday. His habit was to break household tasks up into several groups. This time, he'd done the rug and then stopped for a third cup of coffee. "I have never seen anyone who can just sit the way you can!" she said. She herself worked quickly, focused on scrubbing a counter, picking up magazines, tilting used cat litter with scientific precision into a white plastic bag that she tied into a knot. He seemed always on the verge of pausing even while he worked. "What do you think about, when you look up like that?" she'd asked him. He was cleaning the picture window with ammoniated water, wiping it dry with a wad of newspaper, scrubbing at recalcitrant streaks. He had stopped and was staring through, at the blue spruce, its soft new needles, the long branch he'd have to cut if they didn't want to brush against it constantly when entering or leaving the house. "I don't know," he said. "Don't you like doing this?" she asked. "No, no, I like it. I really do. I love seeing the light come through. Everything so clear. It's like getting new glasses."

"Maybe I should go down myself," she said. "Jeff's closing the store on Monday so he can see his kids in Florida. I can take a few days. I can catch an Amtrak at Stamford. You're at all those damn meetings anyway." When he began to agree—his pulse quickening from too much coffee—she said, "Won't you miss me at all?" He protested that he would.

Sunday morning, before she drove to Stamford, they made love. He made a special omlette. They read the *Times*.

"Just breathe naturally," Norma said.

He was face down, resting his forehead and chin in the rubber mask. She had decided there was one more thing to do. He felt thin wires of heat where the needles went along his spine.

"Oh!"

"What?" she asked.

He lifted his mouth from the mask. "Sorry. It's nothing."
He had in the space of a few seconds fallen asleep, dreaming
that his father was hanging upside down, arms fully extended,
swaying. "Is my face red?" his father said. "I'm bursting! In
the old days, they'd have cut my throat like a chicken." "I
know I'm dreaming," he said. His father, ghastly gray, replied, "You think I can't get inside you?"

Two days ago, Elizabeth's husband had tracked him down at
school, a tall, harassed man, wearing washed-out jeans, a
woolen sports coat, sneakers. He was blond, like Elizabeth,
with the same precision in his bone structure, his profile. He
pointed at Alan and said, "I know what's going on. I just want
you to know that. I know what's going on." And Alan spent an
hour telling him that nothing was going on. He watched the
light fade from the man's eyes.

"Your pulses are much better," Norma said. "Do you feel
any tenderness here?" She manipulated the area of his occipital
lobes, the two ridges of his skull on a line with his ears. Her
hands went down past the atlas, along the medulla, to the
cervical vertebrae.

"No," he said. The prickling in his scalp had ceased. So had
the trembling of his tongue. He listened to the dripping of the
fountain and could hear her children on the other side of the
double doors running up and down the stairs. She told him she
was going up to her attic room, to prepare more herbs and
count out his Heavenly Emperor caplets. There was little more
to do.

Lisa had called from Marietta. She had gone for the first time
in years to temple, with his mother and Aunt Sarah. She
described where it was, near the landmark everyone called the

"Big Chicken" that had been stripped of its covering during a recent storm, so that now, in front of a Kentucky Fried Chicken, it was just a tapering tower of girders with a yellow beak at the top.

"Everyone's fine. You should see Edwin doing arithmetic with Sarah. And we went to Underground Atlanta, and I got these great wraparound sunglasses. I look like a pilot."

"We had a flood," he said, "but the sump worked. It's just a little damp."

"You know what?" she said. "You know what? I took the kit with me. I just had a feeling. You know what?"

On Norma's table, he felt himself falling asleep again, the way he had fallen asleep, after Lisa's call, to the tweeping of peepers down the hill, where the rain had runneled into the wetland, where skunk cabbages proliferated, where teenage boys had thrown beer cans and empty slurpee cups. He'd awakened, his cheeks wet with tears, and dressed and gone down the road, in moonlight, to the culvert and the dying Chinese elms twined with wild grape vines, the peepers making their high-pitched racket. He heard a thrashing in the woods, and saw, retreating through a cluster of black birch, a white flame that was the erect tail of a doe. Then another sound, of snapping twigs, and the stag leaped clear, splashed through water, and lowered his antlers to avoid vines hung from the elms. He slid with narrow hips into the area just vacated by the doe. Suddenly overhead appeared the shadow, then the lit, long body of a blue heron, its wings outspread, too far south of the Adirondacks, too far north of the Carolinas, gliding soundlessly and lost.